ABOUT

CW00405069

James Maher w
He currently re
where he still ho
ment whilst stub........ ....
whenever he physically can. *MoreTwenty4* is
the follow up to his celebrated anthology of
short stories, *TwentyFour7*.

Alana,
IF I shift enough of
these, I promise to get
my own calculator.

MoreTwenty4

Maintaining momentum

James Maher

Thanks for being a
brilliant open plan
office next door
neighbour!

Dan

© James Maher 2007

MoreTwenty4

ISBN 978-0-9554491-1-6

Published by
Showtime Publications
Easthampstead
Bracknell
Berkshire
England

Designed & produced by:
The Better Book Company Ltd
Forum House
Stirling Road
Chichester
West Sussex
PO19 7DN

Printed in England

CONTENTS

ACKNOWLEDGEMENTS

Who said lightning never strikes twice?

Here I am, completing the end of the second book, and you are just about to start it! However, if it were not for the growing, ever loyal support cast who have continually provided me with the endless guidance, feedback, patience, wisdom and personal motivation, this book would not exist.

For many reasons, this part proves to be the most difficult to write of them all. However, *MoreTwenty4* would still be a mere figment of my imagination if it were not for the following people:

Ruth, who once again stayed proudly by my side through the good (infrequent) and bad (too many to care for) times, even when faced with the very real prospect of becoming the next member of the "aspiring writer widows' club". Thanks babe – I love you.

Mum, who has never ever stopped believing, and still maintains the best is yet to come. (Does she know something I don't?)

Nicola, without whose input and hard work the whole thing would fall apart, and for making it all look *so damn good*.

My appreciation must also extend to Iain Robertson for "getting it" from the very beginning, and actively encouraging me to ignore the doubting brigade.

I would also like to thank everyone (and there are *lots*) at WH Smith who assisted me either directly or indirectly in making the first book such a success. Your time, feedback and outright support means so much.

Whilst this book is a work of fiction (it's pretend, believe it or not, I made it all up in my head!) it would be shameful of me should I fail to acknowledge the "special six" who provided me with the inspiration to create the crazy world featured in "Days in Paradise" – you know who you are! Any true resemblance is *purely* coincidental of course …

Finally, I again sincerely thank every single one of you for your support and appreciation. Whether you bought the first one, came to meet me on the tour (I have the pictures to prove it!) or did both, I am grateful beyond expression. As always, the notion that people are prepared to open their purses or wallets to obtain words that tumble from my head leaves me privileged and honoured.

I hope this one meets your expectations. Thank you.

James Maher
February 2007

Readers' feedback for *TwentyFour7*

"Brilliant! When's the next one coming out?"
Karen, London

"Very good … I want to know what happens next, sooner rather than later …"
Christine, Swindon

"Really good … it's great fun for reading in coffee break without having to concentrate too much!"
Jodie, Bristol

"The author has a quirky outlook on the world around him … I couldn't predict the plot turns despite my best efforts …"
Iain, Glasgow

"… Just perfect for a reader with little time, yet likes to read – like me!"
Nisha, New York

"Excellent. James possesses a varied and vast imagination."
Cliff, Birmingham

"… highly impressive …"
Karen, Coventry

"… Eye catching and a brisk read. Clever ideas run throughout the book …"
Robin, Amsterdam

Also available by James Maher:

TwentyFour7:
Contemporary tales for people on the move

For Megan, Aidan and Grace.
Forever.

Inside Information

'Can you move down inside please?' the despairing female voice cried from the platform's edge.

Inside the packed carriage, a silent groan escaped the collective lips of the densely packed crowd. Despite unspoken protestations, the steady shuffle of feet and rustling newspapers allowed the few square inches needed for the agitated woman to climb aboard before the doors closed with a final hiss, signalling the imminent departure of the 19.05.

Safely tucked away at his window seat in the middle of the carriage, Michael Adams was only too aware of the immense discomfort his standing travelling colleagues were feeling.

Outside, the temperature was 95° Fahrenheit. It had been the hottest September on record. All the free evening newspapers now littering London's Tube and mainline stations had screamed that particular headline every day this week. It was hot. Very hot, frayed temper weather.

Despite such discomfort and cramped conditions, no one complained. Not even a tiny sigh or mutter. It just *never ever* happened.

This living hell of being packed like sardines into a tin, and having to pay extortionate prices for the privilege was simply accepted as a fact of life by everyone who braved the daily commute into London. After all, it's where the work is.

Tottenham Court Road station had been a seething mass of humanity upon his arrival fifty minutes ago, and the heat, smell and moisture from the overflowing throng of bodies had been unbearable. Services were experiencing severe delays as a result of signal failure at Epping, so not only did he have to wait for thirty minutes until he actually reached the platform, the journey to Waterloo (once he was ensconced on a train, his face pressed against a door window – of course claustrophobia had not been fully understood until the advent of the Northern Line), had taken three times longer than usual. Whilst on this particular leg of the voyage home, he was powerless to prevent the middle-aged woman behind him smothering his back with her chest and thighs. Despairingly, he made a mental note to write a letter to *The Evening Standard* – after all, men were always being reminded of etiquette riding on these packed sub-terrain vehicles. What about protecting the men who were equally offended by *women* who wanted to cop a feel?

Spilling from the brutally crammed carriage at Waterloo had come as only a slight relief. Upon reaching the concourse, the enormous electronic destination board illuminated the fact he had five minutes to dash across to platform 15 to catch his next train.

Forget it. He would wait another fifteen minutes for the 19.05. Same hell, different day.

Michael mooched across the rapidly filling concourse to the deserted platform 19. In Britain's biggest railway terminus, there was always an advantage to knowing where your train was going to be arriving before its silent announcement on the electronic boards. In five minutes, the platform would be packed, and, as the masses converged on 19, the stampede would be unbearable.

He waited patiently, acknowledging the existence of those other well-informed platform dwellers that could be found here, in the same place at the same time every night.

As the train arrived from its inbound journey, he stood aside, allowing the alighting passengers to spew forth into the unbearable heat of the capital. Once they had disappeared, he immediately jumped on board – Carriage C seat 27 – as with all London commuters, he was a creature of habit to almost anal proportions.

Allowing thirty seconds to settle himself in, placing his holdall into the soon to be jam packed luggage rack overhead, he took residency in his usual seat as the hordes steamed onto the train, filling it to capacity within seconds. Now, as the groaning passengers had reluctantly created room for one more, and the doors angrily snapped shut – electronic airlock, the finest German technology available – Michael adopted his usual routine of taking a good look around him as the train pulled away from Platform 19 (the place where 'Eurostar meets Clapham Junction every hour') with an agonizing slowness that betrayed the certainty every carriage was at least 100% overcrowded. As usual, they were so densely stacked, there would be no guard coming round to inspect tickets this evening. No, he would be sat in his little compartment, afraid to venture out for fear of being lynched (if anyone had the room to do it).

Jostled by the motion of train wheels pounding on metal tracks, the usual suspects gathered. Rumpled suits rubbed shoulders with dumbfounded tourists making their way out of London. Aggravated city types spoke loudly into mobile phones, warning the unseen recipients (usually loved ones) they were going to be late home. It was amazing really, without exception, everyone standing was reading something – usually the men a newspaper, the women a novel.

Above their heads, air conditioning, hummed noisily, having no effect in the stifling conditions.

Craning his neck as far as the conditions would allow, Michael quickly took in the circumstances of the privileged few for this journey – those who had a seat.

Cocooned in their private cubby-holes, they were like royalty; as theirs was the gift of choice. For them, their biggest worry was which remote and distant sanctuary to retreat into, enabling them to ignore the plight of the others without the faintest whiff of conscience crisis. Many of them were hidden behind the shelter of newspapers or books. Equally prevalent were those whose work/ life boundaries are so blurred, they tapped frantically at laptops and BlackBerry devices. A growing army of devotees simply sat with their eyes closed, the thin white cables of their inner ear phones betraying them as carriers of the latest anti-social craze from the other side of the pond, that of the church of iPod. Interestingly enough, in these fast changing consumer led twenty-four hour society times, Michael counted three people simply looking out of the window as the train rolled onwards, pretending to be interested in the glamorous surroundings of such sights as Vauxhall bus station as it flitted by.

Satisfied at the discomfort of those around him, Michael reached into his breast pocket, removing his very own statue of commuter worship, a commonly growing phenomenon known as 'Nano.' Placing the white corded plugs into his ears, he switched the tiny palm sized device on, and immediately agonized over which of the 500 tracks he wished to listen to. It was not as if he liked all 500 songs (only occupying a fraction of its vast memory), he didn't, but he had 500 songs on it because he *could*.

Eventually, as the train groaned into Clapham Junction, he selected the 'random' switch, and settled back into the rock hard upholstery as a blessed number of tortured souls left the body-locked carriage.

Fifteen minutes later, the exotic climes of Richmond were attained, where several more tired and weary troubadours of the 9 to 5 left their worries behind them, within the tinderbox confines of carriage C. At the exact point the doors did their hissing, clicking, locking thing, Michael's troubles started.

Initially, he put the sudden intermittent static intrusion down to the battery, even though he had recharged it the previous night, as he did on all nights prior. Probably just the heat then …

Trundling into Staines, Michael awoke with a sudden jolt. Once again, the commuter angel of darkness had stolen precious minutes from his life, cursing him with the heartache of 'catching fly sleep'. He was not alone, for, on every packed carriage, men and women of all denominations become inflicted with this disease for no apparent reason. Symptoms include lolling heads (either into a window which is painful, or your neighbour, which is excruciating), open mouths (hence catching flies), and, in extreme cases, uncontrollable dribbling.

He had been hexed with the worst curse possible tonight. His head had lolled forwards, and, much to his horror, he had dribbled, resulting in a perfectly round wet patch the size of a coffee mug straddling his chest. Wiping remnants of the incriminating saliva from his chin, he sat up, suddenly taken aback by the deafening static hiss, emanating from the still attached earpieces, assaulting his senses. In the semi mindless fug of part awake, part asleep, it almost sounded like the hiss was talking to him. Almost sounded like it was telling him to 'geeetoffffff …'

How on earth had he slept through that?

Unable to remove his eyes from the monstrosity on his chest, without any way of covering it up, Michael removed the earphones, switching off the Nano. As even more bodies shuffled off the train into the mid-evening sunlight, Michael had no choice. Reaching to the now empty rack above, he brought his holdall down, protectively placing it across his chest. Embarrassment burned his cheeks to the point of blistering.

Lurching onwards in their voyage through the Home Counties, he maintained a tight grip on the brown bag, clutching it to his torso, when a sudden lurch, accompanied by the sound of twisting metal, disrupted the normal routine. The train stuttered to a sudden, shocking standstill. Inconvenienced muttering broke out amongst those remaining in the carriage, their whispers of discontent slowly rising in volume with each passing second.

Several more minutes passed, then the crackling of the on train tannoy scrunched up the tranquillity of the summer air. The nasal, scratchy voice carried across the airwaves betrayed no emotion.

'Good Evening ladies and gentlemen, this is your guard speaking. I am sorry to announce that due to a technical fault on this train, this service will terminate at Egham. Please listen for further announcements.'

And that was it. The train slowly commenced its journey once again, the banging and screeching from below confirming that it was limping into Egham with a mortal injury.

Again, more whispered tut-tutting. The situation was getting critical now. Too much more grumbling and Michael was convinced someone would have a heart attack with the effort of maintaining current mutterance levels.

Painfully slowly, as if the train and world directly outside it had been switched to slow motion by an unseen celestial controller, they arrived in Egham. Chuntering to an agonized halt with metal shrieking and screaming below them, the weary travellers were grateful for the relief to their auditory senses. For everyone concerned, the ringing in their ears would serve as a long-standing reminder of the events about to envelope them.

As silence befell the half empty carriage, the first strange thing to happen was the *failure* for something to happen. From above, the crackling speakers spoke no words, the guard obviously tongue-tied as to explain what was expected next. The electronic door locks remained firmly in place, ensuring their imprisonment aboard the redundant transporter – for the time being at least.

Had the guard died? Surely it was his job to ensure his passengers were kept informed of the situation, as well as allow them access on and off the train? Had he never heard of public safety or the passengers' charter?

Around him, Michael sensed crackling unease, increasing in intensity amongst his fellow travellers. Many were now cursing from behind him. Lamentable calls to loved ones commenced from mobile phones all around. Compensation was already *the* buzzword on the carriage. A large, grey haired gent, his Saville Row pinstriped suit betraying his City of London occupational status, shot up and walked to the doors. He made his bellowed feelings clearly felt – he wanted to get off and make other arrangements, and he 'won't calm down and I don't care who knows about it!'

Sinking further into the isolation of his seat, Michael again pulled the Nano from his bag, unwrapped the white cord inner ear headphones, and hoped for the best. As soon as the 'play' button was depressed, his senses were once again assaulted by the ferocious, uncompromising buzz of indiscriminate static.

Instinctively, he gripped each tiny earphone, yet in the split second it took for him to grasp at them, the static pitch suddenly changed, and a very audible, almost familiar sound broke through the sinister hiss. It was only one word, but was enough to change his state of mind forever.

'Wait!' It was an exclamation, an edginess that betrayed desperation for attention.

Michael dropped his hand, numbness setting in at the alien yet familiar voice breaking through the static. Adjusting the volume to ease the increasing crescendo pounding his inner mind, Michael groaned aloud as another instruction penetrated the now painful, hellish sound.

'Leave now! LEAVE NOW!'

Fear, confusion and uncertainty gripped his sense of rationale as if it were caught in a bear trap. How could this be? Such was his state of anxiety, he failed to notice the swell of movement around him as fellow passengers commenced circulating within the carriage, with several of them converging at the reluctant electronic doors, trying to forcefully prise them open. Beyond the confines of the train, the platform was strangely deserted, even for this time of the evening.

'LEAVE NOW! LEAVE NOW! LEAVE NOW! LEAVE NOW!' screamed the phantom of his inner ear. Michael was convinced his heart would explode in panic and that he could quite literally die of fright. The voice was unmistakeable, and yet this method of contact was totally impossible. He was going nowhere, his visceral anxiety generating a complete severing of brainwave impulses to his limbs. Michael was paralysed in fear.

'How can I leave?' he groaned aloud. 'How can I do as you ask?'

'Quite right mate!' The distinguished pinstripe hollered from the frozen door. 'Bloody electrics have gone and we're trapped in this bloody thing!' His words fell on deaf ears. No one, including Michael was listening. 'LEAVENOWLEAVENOWLEAVENOW LEAVENOW!' Michael jumped at the loud, abrupt command, painful to his delicate auditory senses, yet jolting him from his paralysis none the less.

How could this be? Was he dreaming? 'LEAVENOWLEAVENOWLEAVENOW

LEAVENOWLEAVENOW!!' Frenzied panic pumped through the micro speakers. Michael violently tore them from his ears, desperate to hold on to the voice, yet unable to cope with the disorientating physical pain.

'HOW?' he screamed aloud towards the white illuminated ceiling. 'HOW?' he cried again. 'CAN'T YOU SEE? LOOK AT THE DOOR!'

Now everyone on the carriage *did* stop. As one, they appeared to move away from him by a couple of steps, retracting from this potentially destabilised person now giving them a further cause for concern.

'Calm down, mate.' A cockney female voice floated across the invisible sea of tension. 'I'm sure someone will be along …'

Whoever she was, her sentence remained unfinished as the recalcitrant doors violently hissed open, the force of their parting causing the very frame that housed them to buckle and bend.

A moment of shocked silence preceded major spillage as frustrated commuters poured onto the platform.

With the temporary diversion from the shattering spell of the Nano, Michael gathered his bag, joining the remaining passengers on platform one in a scene reminiscent of *Exodus*.

His heart quickened again once he noticed that every door along the side of the train had been violently ruptured in a similar manner as the one on his carriage. Such velocity and force was beyond the comprehension of any sane person.

Surveying the scene around him, Michael decided the best thing to do would be to stay in the background, and focus on regaining his composure. No one else seemed to be panicking; everyone seemed to accept the inevitability of the situation. Now they were all off the train, a strange sense of calm returned to the faces of those around him.

He had definitely been given a command by a very familiar voice, yet knew it was a complete impossibility. Pondering the implausibility of such an event, his Nano started violently vibrating in his pocket. There was no alternative other than to retrieve it, and either remove the battery, or simply cast it aside.

He did neither, the message on the small LCD display screen put paid to that. Its words were simple yet devastating:

'Put the phones back in … I'm not finished yet …'

The Nano was switched off. No power flowed into the unit. Yet the message was as clear as the crystal blue evening sky. Bringing the micros back, the static was evident before he had even returned them to his ears. However, the sounds were now far less violent.

Closing his eyes, Michael braced himself. His sense of reality slipped away by the second, yet he was powerless to stop himself falling under the spell of the intoxicating situation he found himself in.

'Don't be gone ….' It was the same person transmitting. 'Don't be gone forever. Don't be gone Michael. Don't follow the others …'

'I'm not going anywhere dad,' he whispered as tears of anguish began their descent. 'Where are you? Are you here with me ..?' His question hung in the air, suspended in perfect synchronicity with the stillness of the stifling evening.

The air … something was wrong with it. It felt heavy and … soggy. He could still breathe, yet a strange coppery taste invaded his mouth.

'Don't be gone. Don't follow the others. Don't be gone …' The unmistakeable voice of his father pleaded. It was more than Michael could bear. The sudden loss of his father ten years earlier in one of the worst high speed train accidents on record had wrenched away the very identity of his family – robbing them of the glue that held them together.

'Where are you dad? Are you near …?'

No answer. The static disappeared, yet the words of his father remained a strong echo in his mind. Confusion reigned internally, and the need to breathe came in short sharp gasps. He was clearly being haunted by the spirit of his father, but why? And why now? Fighting the urge to vomit, he sank to his knees, sobbing uncontrollably. No one took any notice – every single soul on the platform was occupied with events elsewhere, namely the events occurring in the sky.

As he lay sobbing, curled in the foetal position on the bare concrete, nearly one hundred complete strangers looked skywards and joined hands.

The light of the evening was invaded by a sudden, abrupt darkness. A rational mind looking in on this scene would have asked some significant questions requiring immediate attention:

Why is no one helping the prone young man lying on the ground?

Where are the train driver and guard?

Where are the station staff?

Why is everyone holding hands?

Why is it so very quiet (except for the young man sobbing)?

Why is there what appears to be a large tear or hole in the sky?

Michael was temporarily forced from his inner torment as his father returned once more.

'Stay, don't follow them …'

'Follow them where? What do you mean …'

Now, he noticed the large rent in the sky, the focus of everyone's eerie, silent attention. It was clearly a hole – a vertical, jagged tear, as if you would expect with a piece of cloth cut by a pair of blunt scissors. Stretching from north to south, it reached as far as the eye could see from horizon to skyline summit. Beyond the tear, a strange shade of bright green hue silently pulsed and rotated. Yet despite this apocalyptic scene, calm and tranquillity resonated across the very fabric of the station, including all those within it.

'Don't follow them … let them go …'

Despite his state of anxiety and confusion, Michael was mesmerised at the sight before him. Yet, the bonds with departed flesh and blood are unbreakable, and his instinct was to obey his father, no matter how diverse from reality this situation was.

Without warning, the tear extended outwards, as if reaching to the very periphery of the station itself. Michael instinctively took a step back as the words of his father echoed loudly in his mind and a shimmering green fog enveloped everything and everyone around him.

He stood wide-eyed in a combination of incredulity and hypnosis. The green mist stopped within an inch of his foot, and, as if warded away by some unseen force, immediately retracted.

Within seconds, the fog lifted, and without noise or fanfare, the tear above corrected. There was no sign of what had gone before him.

Only now, Michael stood on the platform completely alone. The entire station was deserted with one notable exception. Him. Of his fellow commuters, there was no sign. Where a malfunctioning commuter train once stood before him, not even a shadow remained.

Everyone and everything associated with that train had disappeared completely, consumed by the coloured haze. Michael was alone and confused. As he felt consciousness slipping away, the Nano violently shook once more, thrusting his senses back to the frightening, unbelievable present.

Another message appeared on the screen. 'Good Lad ...'

Mercifully, the protective trigger of his rational mind activated, and Michael passed out.

* * * * *

'Don't move my love, you've taken a nasty knock, keep still, the ambulance is on its way ...'

Lying prone and exposed on the grey concrete in the recovery position, feelings of searing pain washed over as he fought to open his eyes. Stinging rays of sunlight pierced his blurred vision, the pain of adjustment to the bright light intense. His head throbbed and bones ached. Instinctively, he motioned to pull himself up, but whilst the mind was willing, the body was unable.

'Try to stay still love; you took an almighty bash on the head as you fell ...'

He briefly, painfully opened his eyes, but only made out the silhouettes of unknown others surrounding him, looking down on his prone figure – they seemed so far away.

'Where am I?' Despite the scintillating pain in his frontal lobe, he was coherent.

'You're still in Egham, pet. The train broke down, do you remember?'

'Yes, of course.' He remembered everything, and in doing so felt cursed by the experience.

'Well, as we were all getting off, you seemed to get some sort of electric shock from your headphones, because you suddenly shook and passed out. You didn't half whack your head on the platform when you fell …'

The sound of the woman's voice, whilst comforting, faded in and out, her volume adjusting with the intensity of pain in his skull.

'Anyway, I've put the small headphone gadget back in your bag love – strong little things aren't they? It was still playing even after it clattered onto the floor. Not a scratch on it. Still, I don't expect playing loud music like that is going to help you either now is it? I mean, fancy listening to a load of nonsense like that! It sounded more like static hiss to me!'

Michael was barely holding onto consciousness as he heard the distant wailing of sirens, and slightly closer, the frantic station announcer apologizing for the fifteen minute delay due to technical problems on the train, 'Which have now been fixed, so could all passengers please re-board the train. We apologise for the inconvenience to your journey.'

Succumbing to the painkillers suddenly injected into his bloodstream by blurry images of men adorned in bright green, his smiling father greeted him as he was lifted into the ambulance. 'Good lad …' he grinned, fading into the eternal green hue, departing once more as he spoke.

* * * * *

The accident was catastrophic. There had been no warning, and driver error had not yet been ruled out. However, there was a great deal of focus on the interim repair work to the electronic braking and emergency exit systems carried out during an unscheduled stop earlier in the journey at Staines. The later editions of newspapers and the late night news broadcasts broke the story to an unassuming nation.

Approximately twelve minutes after leaving Egham, the severely delayed 19.05 commuter express service from London Waterloo to Reading, heading towards Sunningdale, for reasons yet to be established, abruptly derailed at

80 mph. All eight carriages parted from the tracks with the force of impact. Seventy-seven people were on board. One survivor was confirmed, a young male, travelling alone, who, as a result of a suspected heat related illness, had remained at Egham awaiting medical attention.

HateWish.com

Sitting at his office workstation, staring idly beyond the grubby windows providing a generous view of the staff car park, Rory silently counted down the seconds, his mental clock ticking loudly in his mind. Idle chatter wafted across both ends of his work pod, mostly from the unmotivated women who were discussing in great depth their plans for the weekend. Even though he wasn't listening to their disinteresting, stupefyingly boring conversations, he knew that judging by the sporadic outbursts of mischievous, cackling laughter, they were probably talking dirty.

Friday afternoon, 4 pm. It was that time of the week again, that time when everyone was physically present, yet there was no desire to complete any work. Poorly managed and disconnected from their employer's mission statement as a result of the worst line manager in the world, Rory and his all female team of advisors idled away so much of their time these days, they had re-christened themselves 'The Living Dead'. Switched off and zoned out was a phrase that rang true throughout the entire office.

In the past six months, since the arrival of their new, but clueless, disengaging manager, the biggest challenge they faced was to try and look seriously busy until someone actually gave one of them a meaningful assignment. Rory personally felt that he had disappeared from his employer's sight, as if falling down a huge crack in the pavement.

During this intense period of stagnation and decline, the behaviour of Rory and his team had become nothing more than staggering.

All of them had taken at least one day off either sick or AWOL to do something else non work related – without anyone ever challenging it. Sophie, the young administrator had snorted a line of cocaine at her desk without as much as the batting of an eyelid. Inter-departmental office sex had become something of a routine, with couples disappearing to various stationery cupboards and empty conference rooms to make better use of their time. Two of the more senior advisors spent entire days surfing the web, openly talking about it. And, most disbelievingly of all, their boss himself had taken a preposterous two weeks' leave to grieve the death of his pet cat.

The world of industrial insurance had gone completely mad.

Sighing inwardly, Rory watched the fallen leaves from the tree next to his window swirl in a dramatic upwards motion, lifted from their gloom by a sudden autumnal gust. Turning to look at his dull, uninspiring VDU, he was drawn to an unauthorized pop-up that had appeared directly in the centre of his email menu. Such spam was once unheard of within the organization, but, as with everyone else who had been subjected to a sudden and sweeping change of direct line manager following their company's takeover, even the 'secret squirrel' email police had lost interest.

Nondescript in its appearance – white print on a black backdrop – the panel beckoned Rory with a tantalizing invite. *'Congratulations! You can now Change Your Life in 48 Hours on us. Results Guaranteed!'* followed by a much smaller 'click here' in the bottom right hand corner.

Still with fifty minutes to fill before he could officially leave the building (even though no one would notice if he left now), and his emails cleared for the week, Rory absentmindedly clicked the entry icon to the panel.

Immediately, his screen filled with a bright yellow background, headed by large black letters bearing the legend 'HateWish.com.' Centred in the visual was yet more text.

'*Welcome, new user, to HateWish.com. Does your life suck? Is work simply dreadful? Home life a disaster? Money worries? Troublesome kids?*'

Yes to all of the above Rory thought inwardly, stifling a grin. He read on.

'*If yes, then simply register to join HateWish. com now! We will give you the opportunity to enter our monthly 'new members' prize draw, where you're guaranteed a life changing prize! Simply click the 'next' icon to join! Membership is free, and confidentiality is assured at all times. Still not sure? Then click here to read* <u>about us</u>.

Curiosity prickled, hooked by the opening questions that rang a little *too* close to home, Rory obediently clicked onto the 'about us' icon. Once again, the screen suddenly changed, this time to purple text on a green background. As yet, he had seen no pictures or regulatory statements.

'Hi!

HateWish.com was founded in March 2001 by Bryant Freedman from Chicago Illinois. Feeling desperate at the overall state of his work/life balance, he set up an internet chat room for the bored office professionals from the state of Illinois to vent their frustrations about their employers, sharing their desired outcomes, providing humorous light relief in the process. The concept very quickly caught the imagination, and through word of mouth, spread across the entire continent. Within eighteen months, HateWish was a global phenomenon, and continues to grow at the rate of a new member somewhere in the world every seven seconds!

Originally called 'Iwanttokillmyboss.com', the name was changed to HateWish.com in July 2003, mainly due to the inventive retributions submitted for consideration by the millions of subscribers around the world. As the forum developed, so did the span of suggestion, and HateWish.com now covers a variety of topics that go well beyond your boss at work!

Membership is strictly through word of mouth, so you will be reading this having been recommended by a current long-standing member of the forum.

Please be re-assured, HateWish.com is nothing more than a harmless exercise in light relief to ease the burden of the soul destroying, bone crushing existence we know as living in the 21st century. Register now, and after providing us with the most basic of details, you can enter the bizarre, hysterical world of HateWish.com, and see for yourself how your fellow tortured souls out there fantasize away their hours! Enjoy!

To register as a new member of HateWish. com, <u>click here</u>.

Sensing this was nothing more than a piece of harmless fun to while away the remaining half an hour of the week, Rory obediently clicked, wondering whom of his many, many disenfranchised colleagues had already joined and then recommended him.

Once again the panel changed, this time to a standard functional data gathering menu.

*'Welcome to the registration page. In order to provide absolute confidentiality to our members, please enter your details as requested below. You are not requested to provide anything more than a pseudonym as a name – please **do not** enter your real name! Once complete, click the 'next' button, and you are in! Happy Hating!*

Strangely, Rory was only required to complete two pieces of detail – his coded name and his mobile phone number. Nothing else. No addresses, no secret passwords, no intrusive financial questions. Nothing. Quickly, he filled the box with the first codename he could think of, paying no attention to the chatter and laughter of the restless ladies around him.

He typed in 'Roar2me' as his secret name, even though he felt it was naff – it would be only his secret – quickly followed by his telephone number. Once he had clicked onto next, a new cobalt screen flicked before him, eerily illuminating his craggy face.

'*Welcome to HateWish.com, Roar2me!*

You are now a fully registered member of the most exciting, vibrant and relevant electronic mail forum of the 21st century! By way of introduction, you have been automatically entered into our new members' free prize draw, which will take place this weekend!

Now for the really exciting bit! You are now entitled to the special introductory offer of posting your first five hate wishes. Simply click 'next' and complete each box, numbered 1 to 5. Once you have completed, click the 'submit' icon. This will automatically post your Hate Wishes onto the 'global notice board', where you will be able to view the inputs from kindred spirits spanning the entire planet! From then on, simply log in whenever you feel like it, read, and enjoy.

Note: As a result of massive demand, you will be limited to three Hate Wishes per week once you have participated in this special introductory offer.

It's great to have you on board 'Roar2me'! Happy Hating!'

Puzzled yet charmed in equal measures, Rory clicked the 'next' icon, now only having twenty minutes to fill before he could leave. Around him, some of the others had given up waiting already, and were gathering their belongings and putting on coats.

*'Hello there 'Roar2me', please submit your special introductory five Hate Wishes **now!**'*

Grinning, his fingers immediately started busily jabbing at the keyboard, the busiest they had been all week.

HateWish 1.

I wish my wife would shut up and stop nagging me about anything and everything. In fact, I wish that when she opens her mouth to speak, she barks like a spaniel. All she is good for is yapping and growling all the time anyway.

HateWish 2.

I wish my boss had his arse and face swopped over. He might make more sense that way.

HateWish 3.

I wish these bloody lecherous women I work with would stop talking about sex. I wish they were as frigid as a fine coating of virgin snow.

HateWish 4.

I wish my morally corrupt employer to become suddenly and indescribably bankrupt. It would teach those thieving bastard directors a lesson or two.

HateWish 5.

On the point of those thieving bastard directors, I wish nothing but misery and unhappiness on them for the rest of their miserable, shitty lives.

Not the most original or daring entries to make, Rory thought to himself, but a good start. He would spend the weekend thinking up more unique wishes to enter on Monday – when he had nothing better to do.

Using his desk mouse, he guided the arrow icon to the 'submit' graphic and clicked. A new prompt appeared. 'Are you sure?' it asked, with a 'yes' or 'no' option. Without hesitation, he clicked 'yes'. The screen went blank. The terminal suddenly, inexplicably shut itself down. Whilst the LED power indicators on the file server remained illuminated, he was unable to provoke any response at all from his console.

'Sod it,' he huffed. 'It's hometime.' He slowly rose from the chair, reached for his coat lazily slung over the back of it, and left without a second thought. If there was something wrong with the PC, it would have to wait until Monday.

Throughout the entire weekend, he never thought about his new subscription to HateWish.com. Even though somewhere in the back of his mind he carried the notion of dreaming up more inventive wishes, he was unable to give them any time. A constantly nagging wife and two sullen, ungrateful kids made sure of that.

* * * * *

Rory was woken at 5.30 am on Monday morning not by the alarm clock (which was set for a full two hours later), but by the intrusive shriek of his mobile phone text messenger, discreetly placed on his bedside cabinet along with his wallet and keys. Such was the piercing suddenness of the noise; he sat up immediately, disorientated and confused. Next to him, Imelda, his wife of twenty-five years, continued snoring.

Wiping handfuls of grogginess from his eyes, he picked up the offending phone, and gently padded out in his bare feet onto the hallway landing, where he could work out what was going on without disturbing the others. Still woozy, he leant against the main landing wall, clumsily jabbing at tiny buttons to open the message, which now told him it had been sent by an anonymous, unrecognized number.

Who on earth could be sending a text message at this time of the morning? It must surely be an emergency – or a wrong number. It was neither. As the message opened before his bewildered, furiously blinking eyes, Imelda rose, awoken and unsettled by the sudden movement of Rory leaving the bed.

Reading the message for a second time, he blinked even harder. Was someone he knew playing a joke on him? Who would send him such drivel at this time of the morning?

'Congratulations Roar2me! You are the winner of our new members prize draw! You do not need to contact anyone to claim your life changing prize – it's already on its way! Best wishes, from all your friends at HateWish. com.'

Only then in his blurred confusion did he realize no one he knew could possibly have sent the message, as he hadn't disclosed his secret name to anyone. A stern looking Imelda appeared at the bedroom doorway, ready to administer serious retribution for the disruption to her beauty sleep. Rory braced himself as her face scrunched up to commence the admonishment. Then he understood what the 'life changing prize' actually was.

On the third, throat shredding, rasping canine bark that escaped Imelda's lips – her face contorted in complete, total and utter horror whilst placing her hands to her mouth in petrified disbelief – the sickening truth woke him up completely. His prize, and most likely all the other wishes, had arrived.

Never Fade Away

Archie didn't notice the sudden gust of wind come whistling through the tunnel of arching, intertwining branches of the two hundred year old beech trees. It momentarily carried some freshly fallen, crisp brown leaves upwards in a swirling vortex, taking them from the periphery of the grey concrete walkway where they lay, scattering them across a large area of the dewy early morning grass further across the three hundred acre inner city park.

It was a perfect, early November morning, one of the best he could ever recall. Although it was only 8.00 am, the sun hung in a brilliant blue cloudless sky, illuminating the autumnal dew on every blade of grass that could be seen. The air was frigid and crisp, yet not too cold to be uncomfortable. It was that wonderful time of the year when autumn was beginning to give way to the full onset of winter, yet triumphantly resisted by allowing the world to bask in fresh, clear mornings like these.

Sitting on his favourite bench, Archie immersed himself in the world around him one final time. As the schoolchildren from the local primary bordering the south end of the park made their way to the day's lessons, he noticed many of them were in hats, gloves and scarves for the first time that year.

After sixty years of tending to the overall maintenance and wellbeing of the park, it was unsurprising that he was much hardier to the elements by now than many of the youngsters moving before him. What he would regard as a gentle nip could well be felt by others as a distinctly cold snap.

He leant back against the thick wooden bench, digging his gnarled, weather-beaten hands deeper into the corporation issue winter jacket that had been in his possession since his first winter working here. Despite its advanced age, which Archie put at one hundred and twenty years, the bench was still surprisingly comfortable. Smiling to himself, he marvelled at its appearance after all these years. The thick horizontal wooden slats were painted an industrial green – forty-three of the coatings he had applied himself – and the sturdy jet black iron legs remained rooted into the concrete bases three feet below the surface of the soft earth.

'They don't make things like they used to,' he mused inwardly, still amazed he was occupying a spot that had survived two world wars, untold teenage petting sessions, and in recent years, a large, sinister ever-growing volume of mindless vandalism and graffiti.

This was his favoured spot in the entire park. Its origins stretched back two and a half centuries, when the park was constructed by carving out a kidney shaped valley in the marshland that occupied so much of the city. The overall topography gave the park an undulating slope effect.

The park itself, once opened, had many fine architectural features, all of which were now long gone – several of which a broken-hearted Archie witnessed being destroyed – except for the main entry gates at the north end, where three ornately carved concrete pillars remained. Its key characteristics or reference points sat at the geographical extremes. Archie's vantage point at the peak of the north end – the highest part of the park – meant he could see everything – the entire three hundred acres were in his line of sight.

Down at the south end, the school was slowly filling up, and in the next ten minutes, its narrow gated entrance would choke up with the volume of small bodies trying to get through. This had always been the case since 1963, gradually getting worse each year. Whilst still a pleasant building to the eye architecturally, it had been experiencing difficulties of more functional types in the last five years. Teacher turnover was higher than average nowadays, sickness was even higher, and educational standards poor. The kids who did attend were not getting the best start their parents would have hoped for, but such concerns were normal in many schools these days. He sighed heavily at the shame of it.

Craning his neck to the west entrance, the furthest distance from where he sat, the library sat silhouetted in the glow of the early morning sunshine. It was the largest public library in the city, and sat proudly as a testament to learning and knowledge. Once renowned as a centre of excellence, it now faced closure due to the gradual yet alarming decline in use over the past decade.

Shuddering at the thought of his beloved park without the library, he turned his attention to the eastern entrance, five hundred metres in front. It was framed by a pretty Edwardian terrace, which at the time of their construction, would have been the most sought after and upmarket address for miles around. They had been converted into tiny housing association flats twenty years ago, were tendered back onto the private market a decade ago, now owned by an array of landlords who paid scant attention to their upkeep, or the tenants that paid them for the privilege of living there. Subsequently, they were now one of the most notorious postcodes in the city, with a reputation for drug dealing, prostitution and petty crime across the district.

The central focal point of the park was slowly awakening as the wildlife that occupied the small island down in the middle of the old banjo shaped boating lake began moving around the confines of their habitat.

The park was a very popular attraction in Edwardian times, and through the years, as he had witnessed himself on many a summer, the boating lake was the most popular attraction by far. Fed by a natural stream, excited youngsters with their parents would come from miles around to spend a long hot summer's day lazing on its banks, picnics lovingly prepared, soaking up the atmosphere with relish. The lake had two separate areas, one for rowing boats and canoes, and a shallow boundaried area for small paddle boats. All types were hired out to eager users for half an hour at a time.

Even now, Archie could see, hear, feel and smell the sensations of those hazy summers.

He could reach out and touch those memories – so powerful, they would never be forgotten.

In the late 1970s, the lake was drained and unsilted – much of the manual work by Archie himself – and tragically, the boats were removed. Unfortunately, the cost of repair from increasing acts of vandalism had put their private operator out of business. The park had lost yet another institution.

Three hundred fish were set into the new lake area, and now it was the territory of young fishers on early weekend mornings, and occasional model boat enthusiasts.

But for now, the wildfowl had the run of the place. Archie's spirits lifted as the swans, moorhens and ducks noisily filed into the water, stretching limbs and wings, basking in the sunshine whilst it was still there.

Despite the ravages of time, Archie was proud that the children's playground still stood (although the amount of paint needed to cover the almost weekly bouts of graffiti was endless), and that the two tennis courts and immaculately kept bowling greens were still in regular use. It was just such a shame the high fencing and razor wire was needed to preserve their wellbeing.

Archie stood up, his knees crackling and elbows clicking as he stretched his numb limbs. He had been sitting down for a little too long, and his body noisily protested.

At one time, next to the children's playground, there stood a bandstand, resplendent in wrought iron work. When cutbacks in the eighties meant that Archie's team of three was whittled down to one – himself – he could not keep up its maintenance, and eventually, it was demolished. Feeling a failure, he ensured that a raised area was maintained on the site, and, with great effort and dedication, he secured several benches and planted three enormous flower beds. The net result was that band concerts were still held on the site, but only in the two key summer months. With a single tear rolling down his cheek, Archie picked up his small tool bag, and without looking back, headed for the main entrance on the west gate.

Beyond the bowling green, the latest addition to St George's sat. It was the new star attraction. The Skate Board and Stunt Bike area had been erected three years ago. Again, Archie had been in the thick of its construction, despite the fact he was completely against it. He feared it would lower the tone of the place, and he was right.

A concrete and steel construction of ramps, bridges and tubes, it was a complete eyesore, made worse by the explosion of graffiti that occupied every single inch. Archie had never been allowed to move it, as it allegedly 'added character' to the apparatus. Even though it attracted rough sorts late into every night, frightening away the smaller children who wished to use it, the monstrosity remained.

On the morning he found the used syringes tucked in the corner of the small junior climbing frame, he failed to report it to his superiors, instead deciding to go straight to the local newspaper.

The uproar in the following days had been enough to generate some action. Pressure from the community finally forced the council's hand in making a decision.

However, Archie did not count on one particular decision made by his employers. When the suited young man had arrived yesterday evening, Archie assumed it was to update him on the provisions he would have to implement in the Skater Park. Instead, he was told that by a unanimous decision, he was being served notice of his enforced retirement, effective immediately. Fresh, younger blood was needed, Archie had to make way. His time was up.

Leaving the gate for a final time, Archie took his sixty years of history with him. Despite the sadness he felt at the passing of time, he looked forward to new challenges ahead. The first one would be to put sixty years of memories onto paper.

On the back of his exposure in the press, there was an instant clamour for his story by a newly interested public. He needed to get home quickly; there was much writing to be done.

Drawn From Memory

'Gosh! That's a big one for a first timer! Where do you want it to go?' commented the heavily decorated, slightly angry looking peroxide blonde behind the small, almost plastic desk, her smile intense yet perfect, threatening to touch her ears either side.

Malcolm grinned nervously. Sitting atop the home-made counter, carefully drawn upon a pristine piece of heavy cartridge paper, was the tattoo design that had been his personal labour of love for the past six months.

'On my shoulder please.' He helpfully pointed to the area at the top of his right arm, insinuating that the still smiling assistant, whom he knew as Elizabeth, needed a visual aid to highlight where the shoulder actually was. 'How long will it take, and how much?' Malcolm's heart pumped furiously, mainly in anxiety of the damage to his wallet, rather than the violation upon the surface of his skin when receiving the procedure for the first time.

'Hang on love, I'll just check with Andrew. Take a seat for a minute.' Elizabeth disappeared behind a tacky multi-coloured beaded curtain, into the sacred lair of the tattooing parlour – or 'inking' – room itself.

Placing himself on a white plastic seat that perfectly matched the counter, he admired the countless designs decorating the walls of the small waiting area. Malcolm felt a strong sense of relief now he had finally made the bold step of actually coming here. His ultimate taboo had broken as soon as his foot crossed the threshold.

For many years, he had silently admired the intricacies and expertise employed in the culture of body art, despite the stereotypical image surrounding the whole concept of tattooing, tattooists and the kind of people that wear them. At the age of thirty-three, having reached the hallowed professional status of bank manager, he finally decided the time in his life had arrived where it was right – he would take the plunge and 'get some ink'.

Adopting the quest for that one perfect body decoration as a personal project to the point of obsession, he embarked upon many hours of poring through the hundreds of websites and magazines dedicated to the thriving, lucrative industry of professional body art. It was imperative he settled on the design of choice. It had to be no less than absolutely perfect.

Quickly, he learned there was nothing sinister or underhand about the profession at all. Amazingly, those choosing to make a living in applying these permanent bodily imprints could quite rightly be regarded as some of the finest line artists and illustrators in the world. The skill involved in producing them was breathtaking.

'Good morning sir, welcome to Skin Graffiti.' A short, balding, stocky middle-aged man, bespectacled in thick gold rims, stood before him, thrusting his hand forward in a gesture of formal greeting. 'My name is Andrew Matthews, and I'm the owner and illustrator here.'

Wearing only a white vest with beach shorts, Andrew Matthews displayed one of the most breathtaking human tapestries of images Malcolm had ever seen up close before. Every single centimetre of exposed skin was covered in a permanent drawing.

Despite his intimidating appearance, the manner of the proprietor was warm, welcoming and respectful. Malcolm already knew who Andrew and Elizabeth were – the recent features in the local press on their business and clientele were all exceptionally favourable, whether regarding the premises, standard of work or services offered. Following some further 'online' investigative work into the local and national reputation of 'Skin Graffiti', it was clear Andrew's small yet friendly business had regularly gained a top three rating in every survey conducted over the last two years.

'You look just like you do in the papers!' Malcolm smiled, taking in the various trophies and newspaper articles on display in the far right hand corner of the waiting room, almost as if hidden from view to avoid embarrassment.

Upon closer inspection, every nuance of Andrew's skin was a seamless patchwork of dragons, animals, fairies, devils, skulls, tribal symbols, flowers and other varying forms of fantasy art. The man was a picture gallery, a walking advertisement for his trade and his own capabilities.

Andrew grinned back. Clutching Malcolm's design, he got down to talking business. 'Glad you read it! Now, Liz tells me you want *this* on your shoulder, but need a price first.'

'Yes please, I'm on a budget you see.' Malcolm was re-assured by Elizabeth's transmission of his instructions. Her heavily decorated appearance and sharp features, coupled with the severe photographs in the newspaper had made her seem a visually forbidding individual. However, in the flesh, she was warm and genuine. Appearances certainly *were* deceptive in her case.

Holding up the intricate design to the natural light beaming in from a small widow to the side of the waiting room, Andrew took a long hard look at the illustration in front of his client. There seemed to be a small undertone of doubt as he spoke. 'I must admit, it's been a very long time since I was asked to do anything like this.' His eyes never left the piece of paper as he spoke.

'Is it a problem?' A slight pang of uncertainty rasped at the back of Malcolm's mind. However, his words had their desired effect, and seemed to snap the artist from his bout of intense concentration.

'Nah. I can do it for you no problem. Like I say, it's just a peculiar request, that's all.' Removing the glasses from the bridge of his nose, Andrew motioned for Liz to take the design away. 'It'll take three hours, and I can do it for 100 quid. I will need ten minutes to get everything ready and for Liz to trace the line out for me. Is that OK?'

'Perfect.' Malcolm carried the exact amount of cash required, having guessed the procedure would cost him at least a three figure sum.

Afraid to carry any more for fear of losing the wallet or getting mugged, he had decided that £100 would be the limit which he would spend anyway. He produced the ten crisp £10 notes from the wallet, laying them out one by one on the white counter area.

'Right then, I had better get tracing!' Liz beamed. 'Once that's done, I'll put the kettle on.' She cheerily set about her task as Malcolm reclaimed his seat back amongst the thousands of wall mounted designs. Unseen to him, beyond the bead curtain, he heard a radio crackle into life (with some relief, it was the local independent channel's news broadcast, not some headbanging heavy rock racket), and the shuffling and scraping of Andrew preparing the various implements required for the job.

Waiting patiently, heart still thudding, driven by the uncertainty of the unknown, and the absolute permanence of the end result once he walked out of the building, Malcolm's thoughts wandered back once more to the rationale that eventually convinced him to take the plunge. With his research, he had paid a great deal of attention in picking his moment. Gleaning information from the website and newspaper article, there was a clear pattern of trade, indicating the busiest times and when pre-booking would be needed. As a result of this discovery, a quick, old-fashioned telephone call to the shop confirmed that the best time to attend without having to wait would be first thing on a Monday morning. Right now, he was the only person in the place, and the first booking of the day was not for another seven hours, at 4 pm.

The environment was right. Reassuringly quiet, Skin Graffiti was calm, friendly and relaxed with an award winning body artist equipped with the acumen to effectively run and promote his own business, whilst owning an excellent profile in the local community.

'He's ready for you now!' Liz beamed, again displaying those immaculately arranged white teeth. 'Tea or coffee, sugar or milk, or both?' There was a glint in her eye indicating her natural enthusiasm for her profession Malcolm saw in few others in this day and age.

'White coffee, two sugars please.' As she led him behind the counter, beyond the beads, he could not help thinking there was something attractive about her that would stir intense emotion in any man, he just couldn't think of what it was.

Upon entering the studio itself, all thoughts of Liz's mysterious attractiveness dissolved immediately. 'Take a seat, make yourself comfy.' Andrew was once again wearing his rather un rock and roll spectacles, snapping on a pair of latex gloves.

The studio itself appeared identical to a dentist's surgery in nearly every aspect of the senses. A large, blue reclining chair filled the centre of the tiny room. Every surface was insanely clean, whilst the smell of disinfectant and sterilizing cleaning agents assaulted his nasal senses immediately. Adjacent to the chair was a swivelling, custom made tray, anchoring several thimble sized paint pots, countless needle heads and three drill heads. Only missing was the large ceiling mounted spotlight. With thirteen fillings in his head, unpleasant memories of distressing childhood experiences in these chairs momentarily flooded in as Andrew beckoned him towards the chair.

Suppressing feelings of dread and fear he associated with rooms like this from many years ago, Malcolm gingerly shuffled to the chair.

'You OK?' Andrew was perplexed, uncertain.

'Sorry. Fine. It's just …'

'I know, it's like a dentist's surgery in here isn't it? Don't worry. I get that feedback a lot. Now, let's have your shoulder.'

Removing his jumper to reveal a cut sleeve T-shirt, Malcolm eased himself into the chair.

'Right then. Which one?'

'Which what?'

'Which shoulder?'

'Oh. This one.' Malcolm tapped his right shoulder as if needing to inform the tattooist the difference between left and right.

'No probs.' Andrew swivelled around to the other side of the chair, and raising the side arm to gain access to the shoulder at eye height, immediately set about his task, smothering the shoulder with a sterilizing jelly and spray, without fuss or conversation. Malcolm was happy about this, as the more the artist could concentrate, the less the propensity for errors to occur. Liz shuffled back into the room, two steaming mugs in her hands.

'I'm going to man the front now. Is there anything you need me to be working on?' Andrew responded in the affirmative, giving her strict instructions regarding the complex trace out needed for the four o'clock later that afternoon. Once confirmed, she had disappeared behind the whooshing beads, leaving the two men alone in their individual concentrations.

'OK, we've saved a bit of time as the area did not need shaving.' Andrew spoke jaggedly, placing the traced outline onto the now sticky shoulder. 'OK,' Malcolm absently replied, watching mesmerised as his shoulder was prepared for 'surgery'.

'I'm going to do the outline first. That's with a longer needle, and will last about thirty minutes.' He attached the needle head to the hand-held drill piece as he spoke.

'Does it hurt?'

Andrew suppressed a grin. 'Not really, but it *is* the most uncomfortable part of the process.'

The stencil was removed from the prepped shoulder, revealing the detailed outline on flesh for the first time. Malcolm grinned at the sheer size and complexity of it. He could not stop himself thinking of his older sister, who, in a fit of craving for lost youth, had had a small flower etched onto her shoulder for her fortieth birthday. She described the whole experience as 'worse than childbirth'.

A sudden, violent buzz from the motorized needle brought him back to the present with a brutal suddenness. There was no turning back now. The moment had come. 'Here we go!'

He looked on fascinated as the needle penetrated his skin thousands of times a second. Initially detached from the physical sensations in his shoulder as he watched, it took several minutes for the discomfort to set in. There was no pain at all, just a burning, sizzling sensation, as if his skin were being mildly barbecued. Throughout this stage of the process, Andrew worked silently, in a high state of concentration. Stopping at regular intervals to wipe mixed ink and blood from the self-inflicted wounds, the artist's hands were steady and confident.

'Done!' twenty-five minutes had passed in a heartbeat, and the outline was complete. Malcolm was now permanently branded. He marvelled at the raw, lumpen flesh the shoulder had become, delighted with the initial result.

'Perfect so far. Considering it's been a while since you've done one like this, you should be proud.' Andrew failed to respond, his face still picture of concentration as he studied every millimetre of the line.

Once the 'inking in' had started, and the skin sizzling calmed, Andrew gradually became more talkative. Eventually, as the finishing touches were applied, the quizzical artist asked his client of the rationale that had led to such an unusual design.

'I wanted something that represented me and my personality.'

'But something like this? Is that how you want to be seen?' The words were chosen carefully, avoiding offence or doubt now the job was complete. After all, the work would remain upon this man's right shoulder until he was nothing more than dust and bones beneath the ground.

'Yes I do. This is really important in more ways than one. It's not just a picture for the sake of vanity. It's an expression of my self-esteem.'

Andrew raised his eyebrows as a gesture of instinctive bemusement, keen to ask more questions, but decided to avoid that particular path of conversation. Anyway, he was almost done. One final clean with antiseptic spray, a quick appreciation in the full length mirror, and the image was hidden underneath a sterile dressing to combat the initial risks of infection. Andrew took Malcolm through the washing and cleaning routines that were required during the course of the ensuing fortnight, placing particular emphasis on ignoring the need to scratch the wound when it itched, otherwise it may destroy the integrity of the healed image.

Nodding attentively and obediently, Malcolm was determined to follow the instructions to the letter, as compromising the visual appearance of the tattoo would now be nothing short of a disaster.

The two men finally parted with a shake of hands and exchange of business cards. In Andrew's case this was protocol, one, for the unlikely event of an emergency, and two, for spreading positive news by word of mouth – a tattooist's future wellbeing can only be assured by the public exposure of their work and positive reviews from satisfied clients.

With a dull throb gnawing at the top of his arm, but a happy heart, Malcolm left for home; content and self assured he had done the right thing.

During the next fortnight, the tattoo duly flaked and peeled, with Malcolm religiously adhering to the cleaning instructions. As the wound healed, the itch was a distraction, but no where near as infuriating as others had made out. During this period, he was hyper aware of the tattoo's existence and struggled to resist the urge to stop and stare at his shoulder everywhere he went (including at work). There were times he felt as if he were concealing a dirty little secret. Such was his initial paranoia, he took to wearing a white T-shirt underneath his work shirt just in case any of his staff saw his tattoo through the fabric and did not approve.

Being single, he took comfort in not having to justify his actions to a wife or children – he had been far too career minded – but he would have to try to hide it from his mother all the same, as the shock would probably cause her a permanent trauma.

Gradually, some four weeks following the arrival into the world of his tat, Malcolm's paralysing sense of self-awareness diminished, and he got to a point of barely noticing it when catching glimpses of himself. Life returned to normal. So much so, he even found a new project to pursue now his tattoo ambitions had been fulfilled.

At the start of it all, Malcolm set a self-imposed rule of only one body decoration. Despite this, he soon found himself compelled to investigate the possibilities of further tats now he had breeched the taboo of 'having the first one done'. He clearly recalled asking Andrew of the phenomena:

'Why do you have so many? Don't you know when to stop?' Andrew had replied seriously, yet simply. 'It's addictive. Like a drug. Once you start, the yearning for more ink never goes away.'

At the time, Malcolm had taken the comment with a pinch of salt, yet now only two months later, he was trawling as many sources as possible for further designs, sometimes regularly staying up until 3 am as he became consumed once again.

As the urge grew on him daily, he felt incomplete if he failed to trawl at least twenty sources of information each evening, whether it be internet sites, magazines, books or all three at once. Fuelled by adrenalin and raw, visceral excitement, he was soon surviving on no more than two hours' sleep a night.

Amazingly, his work never suffered, such was his expertise and competence. Fatigue, however, was unavoidable. As a result, his reaction to the world around him eroded, losing its natural sharpness. Driving home to what was to have been his seventeenth consecutive night of obsessive design hunting, Malcolm's mind shut down with fatigue, and, falling asleep at the wheel of his car, at 53 mph, ploughed into the rear of the unseen bus, parked at a request stop straight in front of him.

That night, lying in a haze of high dose painkillers and extreme pain in his private hospital room with both legs shattered and a fractured skull, something within the fog of his consciousness concluded he was lucky to be alive.

Charges of criminal damage and failing to drive without due care and attention would be the least of his worries, nor would sorting out the mangled wreck of shattered metal and glass that was once his car. As a drug induced sleep descended upon him, shrouding his senses and swallowing his consciousness, his last lucid thought was of the difficulty he would experience in having to learn to walk again ...

Woozily coming round the following morning, Malcolm was temporarily distracted from his pain and numbness of mind by the most ferocious itching sensation he had ever experienced in his life. Its epicentre was the right shoulder. Reaching out, in great pain, to the sleeve of his hospital smock with his free, uncuffed hand, he pulled the loose fitting garment away, exposing fully his right arm, and with it, the cause of discomfort.

Through his blurred senses, he gasped aloud in horror and shock. Where there should have been a proud image of a recently applied tattoo, there was nothing. The skin was settled, unblemished and free of any abrasion or image. The tattoo simply wasn't there. Not even a remote indication remained of its recent existence.

He fought for breath as the itching intensified. The agony piercing through the hairline fracture as he shook his head in bewilderment caused him to shriek out involuntarily. This was impossible. The tattoo, so personally and lovingly sketched not too long ago was gone. It had disappeared from his body. It was impossible.

Closing his eyes to combat the obliterating pain, Malcolm tried recalling an earlier conversation with his tattooist, as they discussed his chosen image.

Despite his initial discomfort, Andrew did not seem to have too much of a problem etching out the ancient Mongolian warrior design onto his client's skin. Even the bloodstained axe in one hand and the screaming, agony writ, decapitated head in the other did not elicit any sort of response. Yet the image of Malcolm's face transposed onto this warlord from the darkest pit of hell *did* raise an eyebrow from Andrew, even as he was inking the image onto his skin forever:

'Like I said, I haven't done anything like this for years. Pictures of kids and loved ones are quite common, but self-portrait requests are rare, and stuff like this …' he motioned to the original image '… are considered a jinx to those that wear them. Personally, I wouldn't know myself.'

The memory was broken, as panic, pain and disorientation returned with the crashing of the door to his private room. A very agitated and anxious doctor burst in, followed by two dead eyed armed police officers. He groaned aloud at the excruciating violation the noise caused within his fractured mind.

'Mr Wilkes,' she spluttered, unsympathetic to her patient's plight, 'I'm very sorry, but these two men insist on speaking to you right now, and, in light of last night's events, we have decided to give them permission.'

Last night's events? In his state of pain, fear and confusion, he did not even try to respond.

'Mr Wilkes,' the doctor continued tearfully, 'a man carrying an axe broke into the main ward late last night. He destroyed everything in the administration centre, killed the night porter on the desk, attacked three patients as they slept and then escaped through a side window. The police think you may know …' She stopped, visibly wilting under the enormity of the tragedy.

In the blink of an eye, one of the heavily armed, uniformed officers brought his face within an inch of Malcolm's. There was nothing but hate and venom in his eyes.

'We have seventeen credible witnesses say it was *you* Wilkes!' Malcolm felt a loosening grip on consciousness hit him like a smothering tidal wave. 'They've all independently identified you. I'm placing you under arrest for murder right now sunshine. But before I do, you must tell me how you were able to not only escape from your restraining cuffs, or how you put yourself back into them again – but how in the name of all that's good were you able to physically run round the place wielding a quarter ton axe inflicting all the damage you have? Tell me that Wilkes …'

Malcolm felt his grip loosen further still, paralysed with shock, he was unable to move his lips, unable to synchronise his mind to what he was hearing. In that instant, as unconsciousness returned, his soul was crushed, and the foundation of his existence fell apart forever.

'Come on Wilkes! Tell us Jesus, how'd you perform these miracles?'

The officer's words met with no response.

In his unconsciousness, Malcolm could only hear the words of Andrew stating that self-portraits were jinxed. And could only visualise the painfully cultivated illustration of the brutal, savage, uncivilised killer bearing his face, no longer a juvenile fantasy image on his shoulder …

Quiz Night

Once again, Monday evening was a full house at 'The Old Oak'. Even standing room was difficult to achieve without multiple incursions into personal space. Agitated participants in the weekly quiz hustled and bustled, hastily re-arranging the free standing furniture in the main bar and lounge areas of the low-beamed country tavern, ensuring the competing teams sat together, yet in complete seclusion of their competitors. This ritual was played out every week, usually at least two hours before the first question was asked, and always with a high degree of tension in the air. Tonight was no different.

Creatures of habit, all the regular teams usually gravitated towards the same area of the building, sitting at the same tables each week. As the stronger, more successful teams formed their corral of tables at the far end of the thirty foot bar area – unaffectionately referred to as the 'shark pool' by many – the usual arguments flared regarding the proximity of opposing participants. After all, eavesdropping was strictly taboo, and *anyone* suspected of, or caught 'over listening' to another team, would face the harshest of penalties.

Around the amassed ranks of general knowledge protagonists, information freaks, competition addicts and general know-it-alls, harassed bar staff frantically rushed around, acknowledging paper money flapping in the air, desperately trying to keep up with the sudden and overwhelming demand for liquid sustenance from the baying hordes of participants. It was always like this until the thing actually started.

The Monday Night Quiz had been a monster hit at 'The Old Oak' ever since it started eighteen months previously. What were once quiet, mundane, dreary gatherings of only the hardest nosed drinkers in the locality at the beginning of the week, Monday was now *the* busiest and most profitable three hours of trade by far.

Soon after the quizmaster had rolled into town, his unique brand of theatre and engagement had rapidly spread by word of mouth, inflating interest, propelling attendances sky high. Many participants now travelled in from all four corners of the county, happy to spend up to two hours' drive time just to take part, or even be there.

Such was the success and popularity of the format and its compere – known only as 'Master' – the number of participating teams each week had been limited to twenty, with a maximum of eight players per team. Anything beyond these numbers simply broke the capacity limits of the pub itself, whilst the waiting list of hopeful entrants wishing to take their turn counted at thirty-seven teams, increasing by an average of three every week.

'Evening Folks! Welcome to Monday Night Quiz Night at The Old Oak!' the Quizmaster's high pitched, tinny roar blasted out from the sixteen strategically placed amps and speakers dotted across the bar and lounge areas. It was impossible *not* to hear him.

A disquieting hush, a collective sharp intake of breath immediately fell upon the throng as the Master addressed them and the hitherto bright lights were gently lowered. Whilst his tone and pitch were humorous and jovial, the insertion of his dominating voice reverberating from every solid object did little to remove the tense anticipation of that night's participants. Far from it, the start was always the worst part.

Returning to their pre-arranged table settings, the quizzers sat stock still in their seats, hanging on to every word coming through the speakers. The staff let out an over-emphasised sigh of relief now the previously packed bar area was completely devoid of humanity. With the exceptions of the large open log fire crackling and spitting, and the unnerving yet subtle hiss of feedback from the speakers, the whole place had fallen silent. Once again, the next two hours and the stretched emotions of those taking part belonged to Master. He had them in the palm of his hand, just how he liked it. They were all *his* now.

'I'll be coming round in two minutes to collect all your entry fees, and give out the picture round with answer sheets. Make sure you have your monies ready, and pens poised!'

For the princely sum of £1 per player, full access to the depth and breadth of the quiz in all its glory was granted. Starting with a fairly straightforward picture round of ten badly photocopied images, proceedings then moved into ten questions each in the following categories (in order of appearance):

Current Affairs
Food and Drink
Geography
Music

A quirky 'Who am I?' mystery personality round then signalled half-time in the proceedings. Ten minutes later, after the marking of the answer sheets thus far, the second half would start with another picture round, followed by:

Sport
General Knowledge
Nature
'Birthdays'

To conclude, another 'Who am I?' round brought an end to the game. Another ten minutes passed before the final results were announced, and the awards ceremony concluded events for another week.

Such a combination of the Master's dazzling personality and the unique array of prizes on offer were irresistible, and yet, the main purpose for all those competing was purely to register a win, or be crowned the 'Champeens' of The Old Oak for a week.

As usual, the heat generated by the enormous, crackling, spitting log fire, combined with the sheer volume of bodies in the building ensured that conditions were close to stifling. Bouncing around in between the cramped tables, collecting subs in a glass ashtray and issuing paperwork with his customary 'Cheers Folks!' the Master's eyes danced excitedly behind steel rimmed glasses. Beads of perspiration formed on his upper lip, as the first trickle of sweat rolled from his temple, heading in the direction of his jaw.

Slight murmurings continued as he methodically visited each table, not returning to the microphone until satisfied he had collected all his dues. Minutes later, the job was complete.

'OK Folks!' he yelled, shocking the crowd into complete silence once more. 'We're ready to go. As usual, we have one new team, so for their benefit, I'll repeat the rules of the game.' Every week, a new team would *always* enter, as, due to the massive popularity of the quiz, and pressure from the landlord to accommodate every willing participant on the waiting list, the previous week's second placed team had to 'move on and make some space'. After all, the waiting list were a large group of pound signs waiting to happen as far as the brewery was concerned.

Diving into the well-used script for the sake of the newcomers (who already knew the rules anyway), the Master rattled through the structure, format, content and rules of engagement, as the participants poured over the first set of picture round puzzlers, faces crinkled and bodies stiffened in complete concentration. The intensity was already unnerving.

Each team had their own particular and unique name, retained and adhered to every week. Therefore, collective bodies with titles such as 'The Slam Grammers', 'Six Sticks of Dynamite', 'Les Gormes', 'Wamberly Coodies', 'The Mood Scampanions' and 'The Toads' had become part of the widely used quizzers' recognition system over the months.

'As we all know, the current undisputed champeens are the Slam Grammers, having won for the last eleven weeks in a row.' As the great god of the quiz addressed his disciples once more, a collective groan broke the mesmerised silence at the gentle yet unsubtle reminder of the current kings of the block. Familiarity, with too much repetitious winning, bred contempt, even in the genteel world of pub quizzing.

'So, is there anyone out there this week that can knock 'em off their perch? Who knows, they may *even* have to contemplate coming *second* if there is a team out there ready to take them on!' A shudder rippled through the collective.

In the furthest, far-reaching corner of the lounge area, hidden from view to most, a small team of four – two male, two female – eyed each other nervously, speaking to each other only in whispers. The defending, undisputed 'champeens' had been rattled by that last comment from the Master.

'Should we just chuck in the towel for this week? You know, avoid unwanted attention and all that,' the youngest team member, Mark, genuinely asked his companions. Sitting next to him, his mother's response was cut down by the Master's nerve jangling declaration of 'LET'S GO!' and the reading out loud of the first current affairs question. Opposite, on the other side of their table, Mark's father immediately whispered the answer to his sister.

Just as he thought his request had been ignored, question two bounced off the walls, and his father kicked him under the table to catch his attention. With eyes blazing, he hissed the words Mark expected, but hoped he wouldn't hear:

'We go for the win. Absolutely. Just don't dare contemplate second place …'

* * * * *

Placing his mind back to earlier that summer, Mark recalled the time when the Master had taken a four week holiday, to be temporarily replaced by a mere mortal called Dave. His first week had been disastrous. Unexpectedly, he committed the craven act of changing the format, scoring system, and award structure for first and second place. The devastating effect was immediate – a full boycott of The Old Oak until the reappearance of the Master. It was only fair on everyone involved, particularly Dave, who had he been allowed to preside for a second week, would most likely have ended up being lynched by a baying, information addicted mob.

Upon the return of the Master, normal business resumed. As recognition for failing to fill the Master's unfaultable boots, Dave was rewarded with a place on the team of his choice, in order to learn 'how it's done properly round here.' He chose the then reigning champions, a six man group of eggheads called 'Silent Beginnings.'

That very week, inexplicably, they came second, therefore introducing Dave to the unique award structure for first and second place. He personally found out what it felt like to come second, or, as the Master often quipped to his devotees, what it was like to be 'the first of the losers.' Second prize was quirky, yet special, and was the reason why the Monday Night Quiz at the Old Oak was so unique – and so staggeringly popular.

'Concentrate!' his father hissed, pulling Mark from his recollections. 'It's the music round. Get ready!'

Each Member of the Slam Grammers brought their own unique speciality and expertise to the team. For Mark, it was Music and Sport, yet he was also strong on current affairs and the picture rounds.

Shaking the cobwebs from his memories, Mark brought himself back to the present and focused. If it was the music round already, half-time was rapidly approaching, and with it, the first indication of who may not be allowed to return next week.

Five introductions from well known TV themes were noisily pumped out of the crackling PA system, cutting through the thickening cigarette smoke, reverberating from wall to wall. None of them presented a challenge to Mark, who automatically conveyed the answers to his mother, the team's scribe and sacred holder of the answer sheet.

'Are you sure?' The hesitation in her voice confirmed the nervousness dancing in her eyes. 'We can't answer two questions already.

It would be dangerous to drop another one.' Mark noted the stern looks from his father and sister as he caught breath to speak. 'So why don't we just deliberately drop a few more, and finish seventh or eighth?'

To such a competitive gathering, who after all, were his own flesh and blood, this cardinal suggestion of deliberately forfeiting the quiz was met with astonishment, horror and revulsion.

'Are you out of your mind?' his father spat, slamming the heel of his large hands onto the crowded table of empty glasses.

'Impossible!' his sister cried, violently nodding her agreement. 'What's the point of taking part if we don't go for the win?'

As another five introductions were played to the crowd – this time the 1980s – Mark's mother remained silent, attentively noting the immediate answers he was providing, this time unchallenged. Her hand trembled slightly as she filled the gaps across the pre-printed page. It was always the same, yet even Mark sensed it was going to be a close one tonight.

Upon completion of the music round, guaranteeing ten points towards their final total (which they may later regret), the first

'Who am I?' round yielded a concerning return of only three points out of five. Their hesitation, followed by internal conflict in agreeing their first answer for maximum points, had cost them dear, epitomising their mindset completely. Mark sensed it in every nerve and fibre. They were going to lose their champion status tonight, for sure.

Third place at half-time was a dangerous place to be. Even more so tonight, as only one point separated the first three teams. In First place were the Wamberly Coodies, followed by Les Gormes half a point behind. With the Slam Grammers in Third, another half a point behind, the remaining thirteen teams were all at least seven full points behind the top three. As far as anyone could recall, this was the closest half-time gap in months. A sharp, collective groan engulfed the competitors as the realization of the situation hit home. A strategic game of cat and mouse would now occupy the second half, as the three teams at the top engaged in a battle of wits and nerve to establish who would avoid being crowned 'first of the losers' for the week.

'OK folks! Let's plough on with the second half of tonight's proceedings!' the Master boomed. 'It's tight at the top, and a real nail biter is on the cards! Hold on to your seats … let's go!'

As ten history questions were relayed parrot fashion to the newly silenced crowd, Mark shrunk back in his seat, as a look of panic etched itself upon his father's face. Ten questions on the Turkish Empire were clearly not the forte of the teams resident, self proclaimed, history expert.

'If you're not sure, just don't answer any of them!' Mark pleaded. He thought he could feel his parents' sense of inner turmoil. It was completely against their principles to 'take a dive' and lose on purpose, but answering fully when unsure of the proper answer ran a real risk of coming second.

'We will not forfeit this quiz under *any* circumstances. Do you understand?' His father was once again in control. 'How stupid of you to even suggest it!' his sister bleated, herself clearly aligned to the sheer absurdity of the situation. A collective look of resentment emanated from his family, pinning him to the seat. The decision was made. It was win or bust, no matter what.

Anxious looks were exchanged following the history round, as only eight of the ten questions were confidently answered. Yet despite his reluctance to participate further, Mark easily reeled off the ten correct answers in the sports round – the thought of providing deliberately incorrect responses not even crossing his mind, such was *his* natural competitive instinct. Tackled with equal confidence and enthusiasm by his sister and mother were the general knowledge and picture rounds – which unbelievably, involved identifying characters, form a popular 1980s children's puppet show.

Tensions had noticeably eased as the final 'Who am I?' round was announced, and, this time a maximum five points were delivered as all four of them unanimously agreed on the identity of a famous opera singer, best known for one particular concert.

As the Master collected the answer sheets from each team, nervous chatter seeped into the warm, smoky air. The most exciting part of the evening – the reason why the Old Oak quiz was the talk of the county – was upon them.

Slowly, deliberately, the Master dramatically announced the answers to each second half question, pausing for dramatic effect between every sentence. Simultaneously, twenty-four quizzers from three teams conducted the mental recall on how many correct answers they had submitted. 'We only got two wrong.' There was no excitement in his sister's voice, only concern. 'No, I think it was three,' his father muttered, all trace of competitive edge now erased from his voice.

Around them, a final surge to the bar area was under way, from thirsty competitors who once again thrust the bar staff into a state of anarchy and chaos, struggling to cope with the simultaneous demands being yelled at them by the frantic quizzers, desperate to retake their places in time for the announcing of the results.

At separate points within the crowded lounge, three teams sat quietly, unmoving, unspeaking, carrying within them a mixture of anxiety, fear, uncertainty and excitement. Being crowned champions at The Old Oak was an immense feat, widely recognized on the local pub quiz scene as the biggest prize of all. Failure brought tension, antagonism and regret.

'I'm sure we got the half point for question 71,' his mother whispered, half certain, half hopeful. 'What difference does it make now?' Mark retorted. 'Let's just wait and see.'

Under the strict instructions of the proprietor, the Master waited patiently for every glass to be replenished by the overwhelmed bar staff, every penny had to be registered through the ringing tills, and every backside returned to every seat before proceeding with announcing the results. As he waited, the Master patiently prepared the evening's prizes.

Finally, the last contestant – a rotund, dark haired lady wearing a brown T-shirt bearing the legend 'I'm so perfect it hurts,' – resumed her seat, gripping her pint of lager so tight her knuckles were white, sighing breathlessly in anticipation. With a dramatic 'Ladies and Gentlemen … I now have this week's results!', complete silence befell the tavern with the high impact force of a head-on car collision.

Mark looked on calmly as those around him nervously fidgeted and fumbled in their seats. Following his standard format, the Master commenced the announcements in reverse order, slowly in monotone. The first low scores were met with exasperated groans, forced laughter and a healthy sense of relief. For those failing miserably in their quest for a high score, the obvious sense of burdens being lifted was so acute, all those present could almost taste it.

'And finally folks, we move into the top five ….' There was a collective holding of breath, as hearts simultaneously stopped beating.

'In fifth place, on 67 points, we have the Mood Scampanions!'

His sister raised her eyebrows in excitement, or, as Mark was beginning to sense, was it alarm? 'It's a high scoring night,' she whispered, as the others around the table silently nodded in concurrence.

'In fourth place, on 70 points, it is the Wamberly Coodies!'

A very high scoring night indeed, Mark mused, noticing that his father had now crossed his fingers, lowering his head to stare at his feet. Hush befell the crowd once again.

'In third place, on a whopping 74 points…' The pause was deliberate, 'Six Sticks of Dynamite!'

Disbelieving gasps ricocheted between the walls. No team had *ever* gone beyond 73 before. And now, it was a two horse race for the top prize.

His mother placed her head in her hands, and, in a gesture of solidarity, despite his protestations all evening, Mark reached over the table and placed his hand in his sister's. She closed her eyes in response, unable to prevent a solitary tear escaping its shielded prison. Within the hushed, excited chatter, he could hear his father muttering to himself. 'Oh God, Oh God, Oh God …' he chanted, still staring at the floor.

Mark was unable to control his now thundering heartbeat. Why had it been so bloody important to win again? Couldn't they change tactics just for once? However, despite all their disagreements, whether first or second, they had posted a record score. And yet, if they had not won …

'And finally, the two positions that matter!' The Master's voice bristled with a slight yet sinister undertone, any previous joviality diluted by the impending commencement of the prize giving ceremony. A silence so complete, so utterly paralyzing, befell the entire building.

'In first place …' the pause was even longer. '… on a whopping, unheard of, record breaking 83 points …' yet another gasp of disbelief escaped and rebounded across the hallowed walls of The Old Oak, accompanied by a low, murmuring chatter.

'Breaking all records as we know them…' The tension was excruciating. '… but only winning by half a point in our most fiercely contested evening ever …'

He felt numb, the voice of the Master becoming dimmer and distant with every word, yet Mark managed to hang on, kept conscious by the crushing sensation in his hand as his sister gripped with all her might. His father visibly sagged. Coming second on 82.5 points would be nothing more than outright cruelty.

'But a win is a win regardless …'

The other team yet to learn of their fate, a usually cocky group of six young men called 'Les Gormes' were gathered around their table, gripping the rounded edges, sweating profusely with their faces contorted in grim concentration.

'So congratulations to this week's winners …'

Mark verged on passing out, his mother shook uncontrollably.

' … for the twelfth week in a row, with a record score to match their record run – it's the SLAM GRAMMERS!!!'

A female scream pierced the silence in the split second following the announcement. 'But they're so young!' A whispered muttering floated across the room from nearby. Chaos erupted – as was the norm at this point of the proceedings.

With unquantifiable relief coursing through their veins, Mark and his family embraced. It had been a close call. Too close. Tears of relief flooded from his parents. His sister sat quietly, contemplating their lucky escape from the dreaded runner-up spot.

'Congratulations Folks!' the Master had appeared from nowhere with their £20 winnings. 'Mustard stuff!' His jollified pitch and tone had returned, despite the furore around him. 'See you next week!'

'Maybe,' Mark muttered as the Master jauntily bounced back to the front, weaving his way through the nervous animated chatter of the now highly animated crowd. Upon reaching his stage, the Master reached for the second prize, and, once again, his artificially amplified voice reverberated throughout the room.

'OK Folks, as we all know, the second placed team automatically qualify for the first of the losers' prize, which, as we all know, is their loss of registration ...' pausing for a response, he caught sight of the anguished losing sextet, sobbing animatedly in the rear.

'Now ...' the Master continued in a friendly schoolteacher manner, '... I'm guessing that many of you are thinking something along the lines of 'They scored 82·5 points! How could they possibly lose their registration?' But ... rules are rules, and we all signed up to them.'

Mark felt sick to the pit of his stomach, and yet, understood and accepted as inevitable what was about to happen. Meanwhile, the master continued addressing his disciples.

'Next week, a new team will take Les Gormes place, so, as is our usual custom, lets give them our good, old fashioned, Old Oak farewell!' Once again, eerie hush cloaked the seemingly darkening room. 'Lads – if you would come up to the front please ...'

Six petrified young men – average age twenty-two – slowly shuffled to the front as requested. They knew the rules, knew the risks of coming second. At that age though, this particular outcome had not even crossed their minds. Their pigeon steps were met with a mixture of cheering, clapping, sobbing, outrage and distress. Les Gormes were a very popular team, having participated right from the start. Because of their 'old hand' status, they had no choice other than to accept their fate, taking it in good grace, honour and dignity, as had the countless others who had gone before them.

Lining up side by side, shoulder to shoulder before the Master, they exchanged frightened glances as the cheering and handclapping grew louder, drowning out any dissenting voices. Despite their popularity, this was still the highlight of the evening for the vast majority of those who came along. Everyone in attendance was now transfixed – as if hypnotised – on the Master's every move.

'OK lads. I'm sorry about this ...' the Master looked each of them coldly in the eye, betraying no emotion, '... but rules are rules ...'

The Master felt nothing but elation as he reached behind him for the sawn-off double barrel rifle.

'It's time for me to rescind your registration ...'

All six men sank to their knees, numb with fear, yet comforted the end would come quickly.

Unhesitating in his action, the Master deftly pulled the trigger, as one by one, he ruthlessly exterminated the existence of the second placed team from point blank range, their registration permanently revoked.

As their riven bodies crumbled to the floor, the baying and cheering of the crowd intensified. Next week, there would be a group of new faces to play the game.

Removal of the slain corpses commenced immediately, as, once again, the overworked bar staff went about clearing up, as if the bloodied, lifeless bodies were nothing more than crumpled cigarette ends in an overflowing ashtray.

The Slam Grammers quietly slipped out, having bade the Master a quiet 'goodnight' as he wiped down his tool of destruction, placing it lovingly back into a navy blue sports holdall. Once outside, bathing in the freshness of the cool crisp air, it was Mark's mother who triumphantly broke the silence. 'Well … that was a close one!' she grinned, face illuminated by the solitary flame of her lighter whilst igniting a victory cigarette. They silently nodded their agreement.

After such a night of high emotion and excitement, the fifteen minute walk home would be good to clear their minds of the intensity of competition. Whilst the others briskly paced on ahead, Mark lagged behind, replaying the evening's events through his mind.

He decided there and then. No more. It all ended now. He had one week to find an alternative venue with an alternative quiz and alternative host. Somewhere where the prizes were more in line with standard convention.

The clock was ticking.

On the Road Again

He sits quietly in the raised gantry, jaded, but not exhausted. That would be dangerous – after all, he is only halfway through his day. Below, from his position of exulted elevation, the hall fills with studded leather jackets, faded denims, tattoos, beards and assorted bodily piercing. Their clothing boldly proclaims the supremacy of various rock bands that have influenced generation upon generation.

He smiles inwardly, emotionless with nothing but a cold feeling inside. After all these years, they never change.

Within the swelling crowds, there are women in their middle years, ill advisedly pressured into wearing clothes that are too small and far too unflattering for them. Teenagers mingle with fellow comrades old enough to be their parents. In fact, some of them *have* come with their similarly devoted parents. There are bank managers and accountants unleashing the beast within, doctors and teachers eagerly anticipating the arrival of their heroes.

The lights dim, and he assumes position, adorning his industrial ear defenders – an essential piece of equipment – one final time. He flicks several switches in unison, and the first clouds of dry ice emanate from the stage, bathing the front rows of the frenzied gathering in tasteless, harmless theatrical smoke.

As the first beats of bass guitar reverberate across the walls, the rabid screaming commences, and the gig opens with a cataclysm of noise that cannot solely be contained in one room, so it leaves the crowded concert arena, ripping its way through the main doors, tearing through the high street and surrounding areas outside before smashing its way back inside. Once again, a perfect start.

It is his crowning glory, his legacy to the world. 'Murder 1ne' is the world's loudest rock band, and it's all down to him. Fifty massive speakers, stacked floor to ceiling either side of the stage, are blasting 60,000 watts into the audience and another thirty speakers are aimed directly at the band. Twenty microphones are pointing at the drums alone, and a further twenty-five are picking up the rest of the cacophony across the stage. Right now, as the ecstatic screams of ten thousand adoring pilgrims of rock are being drowned out by the 150 decibels being pumped out by the four musicians on stage, the very edges of human auditory tolerance are being pushed beyond their limits. At least half of the massive audience will experience temporary loss of hearing as a direct result of tonight's events. A smaller, unfortunate handful will have a more permanent souvenir of their evening, involving prolonged treatment, with a 50% chance of permanent damage.

Once the first, angry, thrashing four minutes of the opening number is complete, he is satisfied everything is in place. The gig can continue to its conclusion whilst he starts the second half of his day.

Slowly descending the narrow rope ladder returning to the welcoming hard ground behind the stage area, or 'viper pit' as it is affectionately referred to, he joins his similarly ear defended colleagues within the loading bay at the rear of the building. There is no point in talking. Immediately, they set about their work – loading up had already started as the first thunderous guitar riffs scorched through the air – applying themselves with the same crazy intensity as had always been the case for the previous twenty-five years and seventeen tours. His entire existence has been of twenty hour working days of relentless action, leading a team of twenty-one roadies manhandling fifty tons of sophisticated equipment in and out of each venue. However, the mention of their profession as 'roadies' would be met with derision. In this day and age, 'roadie' did not cover the half of it. He is a highly qualified sound system technician, and as such, a skilled engineer in a very specialist area.

They have been together since the very early days. Cramped vans, endless hours on the road between venues, flea hole pubs and working men's clubs at the back of beyond, little or no money and even less security, right through to the packed stadiums and arenas of the world, multi platinum sales, mansions, drugs, booze, accountants, lawyers, women, line up changes, creative differences and various misdemeanours with law enforcement agencies around the world.

Once again he smiles – by rights; they should all be dead by now. Such was their lifestyle of excess, they should all be dead twice. They had him personally to thank for many things, survival for one, but also much of their success. For it was he, through his very specialist technical skills and knowledge, who had enabled 'Murder 1ne' to bestow such magnitude of volume upon an unsuspecting world, catapulting them to the mega-stardom and riches they now take for granted.

In those early, almost prehistoric days, the pursuit of wealth and material benefit had been the furthest from all of their minds. It had been about the lifestyle. He lived for the chance to say the immortal words 'I'm with the band' on a nightly basis. He did it because he loved the glamour of it all, the access to the women (initially the groupies who patiently waited, but the advent of success meant various paid hangers-on bringing willing participants to them), being in the van, tour bus or aeroplane, the after show parties and all that went with it. Within the maelstrom of excess, he also recognizes his professional worth to the travelling circus, the knowledge that he provides them the expertise and know-how to help make them what they are now.

It would take more than three hours to fill the trucks, and their bus was due to leave at 1 am. They would then be woken up a few hours later, in another faceless town, shattered and sore, yet ready to 'rig up' for a show later that evening. Then they would do it again, and again, and again.

Except he would not be with them for that next trip to nowheresville. No one else on the tour party knew it, but enough was enough. The lifestyle meant less as the years took their toll. With his professional legacy assured, it was time to move on.

No one ever spoke of 'what happens next?' The very thought of life beyond the parameters of this pampered, cuckolded existence with the band nothing but taboo, its mention no more than heresy. For him, it was time to find out.

There had never been a solid relationship; life with the band simply disallowed it. No children walked the planet who he could call 'son' or 'daughter'. No bank account with savings existed, no property portfolio or assets to fall back on. Salary was a myth; payment for services provided always came at the end of tour, in cash, and always depended on how well that tour actually did. In the wilderness months between tours, a world of rented accommodation and poorly paid manual labour was the reality. Payment protection plans, ISAs, AVCs and pension plans were a fantasy belonging to others. And now, after thirty years of the fabulous life, he approached his fiftieth birthday with nothing more than damaged hearing and financial ruin to look forward to.

And yet, despite the uncertainty that faced him in the real world, 'what happens next?' had been forced upon him. As the raging torrent of sound continued to abuse the senses of the willing participants in the hall, threatening to crumble the walls around them, he knew of the folly hovering above all of them.

In every aspect, despite his shabby existence and lack of support from his paymasters when not touring, he enjoyed exclusive access to the inner sanctum of the band, a trustee who had been there from the start, someone who could be exposed to anything and everything, no matter how sensational or sensitive.

Several hours later, the final encore smashed through the roof, and ten thousand delirious rockers spilled into the night, savouring every second, ready to regale each other with their chosen highlights, once hearing had returned to normality. Simultaneously, the final truck of the evening was loaded; its massive cargo door slammed shut and bolted. As the juggernaut slowly creaked and rumbled away from the venue, the crew bus loaded its exhausted human cargo, ready to take the shattered occupants on to their next venue.

He told the driver to go on without him; he would wait for the morning truck crew. He wanted to make sure this evening's stage gear was all accounted for – after all, tomorrow was the final night of the tour. Familiar in dealing with such due diligence, the bus driver and road crew bade their farewells, grateful for the respite their trip would provide.

Waving sagely, he had no intention of waiting for the early morning crew. He was leaving right now, without ceremony, without fuss. Bitterness coursed through him, driving his thoughts and actions. Taking one last glance around the cavernous loading bay, he recalled the conversation of the previous evening, when his final band meeting would unknowingly bring the sky falling down around his ears.

'It's like this Joe ...' the world renowned, iconic lead singer said before he even had the chance to sit down. '...we can't do this any more ... I mean ... what I'm trying to say ...'

The news was obviously not good. Spit it out man he thought to himself.

'Well, basically, this will be Murder 1ne's last tour. Ever. We've unanimously decided we can't carry on. We will announce it on the website once the last date has been played. We don't want to cause too much upset before the final gig – it's important from a publicity perspective that it runs smoothly.'

'May I ask why?' he heard himself say, mentally dislocated from the words tumbling out of his mouth, his mind splintering at the impact of such a sudden and shocking revelation.

The response was delivered intensely, gravely, as a very clear matter of fact. 'On environmental grounds. We cannot condone the contribution we are making to the destruction of the atmosphere any longer. We're calling it a day for the sake of the planet.'

'You're joking!' he spluttered.

'We're deadly serious.'

'So you're telling me that 'Murder 1ne', the baddest, loudest band on earth, the band that has kept the industries supporting the audibly impaired in gainful employment for so long ...' He paused, stunned at the incredulity of it all. '... is quitting touring because you want to save the world?'

'That's right.'

And that was where the conversation finished. He left the dressing room with no apologies, no thanks, and no recognition.

Since then, 'what happens next?' had occupied his existence for every minute, every second. He considered himself betrayed at best, discarded like an unwanted Christmas present at worst.

Without hesitation, he walked into the cool night air, making his way to the front of the building. Joining the massed throng making their exit, mingling anonymously, silently, without emotion or regret, he still managed one final smile to himself. Where he was going, he did not know. How he was getting there, he was completely undecided.

In twenty-four hours' time, the loudest band in the world, at the start of their unannounced final ever concert, would be struck mute by an enormous technical failure. A pre-planted technical failure that could only be corrected by one person, a person who would appear on one of the giant screens that hung from the arena ceiling, delivering a message recorded the previous evening, informing the betrayed thousands in attendance of why their heroes had been struck dumb, and why their silence was not temporary, but for ever.

The Guardian of Tangrad

'Never, *ever*, trust anyone,' John Woodruff barked at his trainees, eyes bulging wildly as he spoke. 'Just because you think you know someone, you don't. You are fooling yourself.' He paused for dramatic effect as the small group of six fresh-faced graduates looked up at him. Upon the raised lectern, looking down on all he surveyed, a great sense of importance surged through him.

'Furthermore!' his booming voice bounced off the walls of the deserted atrium. 'You are all so naive; it is highly likely that you don't even know your own true selves yet!'

Among his bemused, mildly intimidated audience, Nathan Polk felt such dramatic statements of suspicion and misplaced identity were a little over the top – after all, Woodruff was only the head of telesales, and they were only under his command for six weeks as part of their grad placement. He also couldn't help but wonder why they had been brought into the huge lecture theatre, when a small room and one desk would have served its purpose much more obligingly. However, on first impression, this guy Woodruff was quite possibly mad.

'Any questions?' Woodruff broke his self-imposed dramatic silence.

It was Adele Parks, the most naive yet academically gifted of the group who walked into the trap.

'Um … yes. Sir, I mean Mr Woodruff …'

'Very well, spit it out then – but be quick! Time in here is costing money out there.' He raised his eyebrows to the exit door, which in turn led to the Mecca of his professional career – the telephone pool.

'I'm really sorry sir, but I … I …'

'Yes Adele? Come on …' His face began reddening with impatience, eyes rolling skywards. He obviously had better things to be getting on with.

'I don't really understand what you mean, or its relevance in working for Sheen Star Life Insurance Services.'

Nervous giggles fanned across the empty room, relieved that this lunatic was now going to exercise his full, slightly askew wrath on the weakest of their group.

'I see … I must congratulate you on your bravery Adele, at least you are prepared to take a risk to gain clarity. I like bravery in a person.'

He dragged his words carefully, looking for dramatic exposure. 'Well, let me put it to you simply.' He remained calm, making the new recruits nervous. They braced themselves for another eyebrow singeing outburst.

'Within this room, one of you is not who they say they are. This is not a wild accusation, it's a fact. The problem is …' he paused, eyeing up each one of them as he slowly paced the floor. ' … the deceiver among us probably has no idea themselves.'

His words caused a faint ripple of concern. This so-called expert, this stranger, spoke in a language that was at worst threatening, at best amusing if not deluded. Yet he was also their mentor at the start of their professional lives.

An uneasy silence descended upon the lecture theatre as master and students reached a verbal stalemate. After five minutes of complete silence, Woodruff broke the deadlock, pressing a small intercom button on the side of the lectern. Immediately, the main double door crashed open, framing an officious female secretary, silhouetted by the artificial light beyond the confines of the theatre. Beyond her slight shoulder, Nathan could hear the distant sounds of chatter and movement as the thousands of established employees made their way across the main atrium to various meetings and seminars in rooms just like this one.

The corporate headquarters of Sheen Star Life Insurance Services was brand new, palatial and vast – a futuristic vision of glass and reinforced concrete. They were the top employer of choice in the personal insurance trade – it was nothing short of what you would expect of the world's biggest company for the markets it operated in.

'Miss Tavares,' he growled, wide-eyed and throaty, 'Please escort the new intake to their work stations.'

Relieved to be getting away from this man who made them feel so uneasy, all six stood in unison, eagerly shuffling from their desks, happy to make their way to the fierce looking blonde with the clipboard poised under her chin.

'NOT YOU MR POOK!' Woodruff bellowed, causing the others, including Miss Tavares, to jump nervously. Nathan slumped heavily into his chair, as if stuck by a lightning bolt. His heart raced, unsure if he would be safe alone in the room with this lunatic.

As Woodruff slowly extracted himself from the lectern, gliding down the steps towards the desks, Nathan had already decided to quit as soon as he left the room. 'That's if I get out in one piece,' he thought to himself, genuinely concerned by the strange behaviour of his employer.

The double doors slammed shut, blocking out the world, sealing them in. Despite the size of the room, which seated sixty, Nathan suddenly felt edgy and claustrophobic.

Woodruff slowly placed himself at the desk next to Nathan, turning in a deliberate right angle movement to look him directly in the eye. As he spoke in his low growl, Woodruff's eyes never left Nathan's, as if he were trying to bore deep into his soul.

'Do you know who I *really* am Mr Pook?' he brought his face so close, Nathan felt short nasal breaths against his prodding chin.

'I don't know what you mean Mr Woodruff. But I do know that you are somewhat scaring me, sir.' He held firm, maintaining eye contact, hoping that the madman before him could not distinguish the tremors in his speech.

'You can cut the Mr Woodruff nonsense Nathan, we both know that's not my real name … don't we?'

As his heart beat frantically in panic, smashing against his ribcage, Nathan struggled to keep his composure. Looking at the door longingly, he contemplated an immediate escape. Consequences to his career were the last things on his mind whilst in the presence of this madman. As if reading his mind, Woodruff spoke again.

'Don't even think about making a dash for it, I will put a Gramayre Ward on you faster than it would take a Dryad Queen to fall from a tree.' His voice was calm and authoritative.

'What?!' Nathan screeched, panicking with a sense of fear he had never experienced in his life before. Yet, as he tried to stand, he could not move.

'What have you done to me?' he screamed. 'Who and what are you?'

In the blink of an eye, Woodruff's features visibly softened, causing him to appear almost normal, even rational, for the first time that morning. He spoke again, this time in ambient tones, knowing he needed to calm the situation.

'I have to say, Nathan, the corrupt fae have gotten a lot smarter in recent centuries. Mind wipe has become something of an occupational hazard for me.' He put his hands to his lips, motioning for quiet from the young man before him.

'I will explain everything, but you need to listen carefully to me. You have no choice. Do you understand?'

This time it was Nathan's turn to look on in muted wide-eyed concern, yet if he was going to get out in one piece, he needed to comply. Reluctantly, he nodded in the affirmative.

'Very well. My name is not John Woodruff, and I do not work for Sheen Star. My name is Ysgengt, protector of the ancient gemstone Tangrad.'

He continued, ignoring the look of complete jaw dropping shock from Nathan.

'The Tangrad is the Key, or portal to the ancient world of Sidhle – the dwelling place of an ancient yet beautiful race of fairies. Over the millennia, Sidhle has coexisted in perfect harmony with Earth, mankind completely oblivious to its existence.'

Transfixed to his chair, still unable to move, Nathan genuinely felt fear for his life.

'Until nine centuries ago, Sidhle was populated by three dynasties of fae, or fairies, namely the Dryads in the North, the Sprites in the South, and the Selkies in the vast oceans. However, this harmony was shattered by the Dryads, when, they decided there were untold riches to be made by exploiting the existence of Sidhle to mankind … For centuries here on earth, humans have always debated the existence of fairies to the point of obsession. The Dryads decided to make contact with dangerous yet powerful men that walk this planet, senior men who lead vast armies. In sharing a common goal of greed and power, they brokered a deal.'

'What has this nonsense to do with me?' Nathan screamed. 'Where did you escape from?' 'HELP!' he screamed at the top of his voice, forlornly hoping someone on the other side of the door would hear him.

'It has *everything* to do with you. You just don't know yet. Allow me to continue.' Woodruff cleared his throat.

'The Dryads agreed to provide mankind with the access point into their realm – the Tangrad – in return for unlimited access to the gold reserves of planet earth, the elixir of eternal life for any fairy. Similarly, by gaining access to Sidhle, the holders of the Tangrad would forever be *immortal*. Can you just imagine it? Every single member of the human race immortal! Alive forever!'

Woodruff suddenly stood and briskly marched to the thirty foot wide projection screen at the back of the room.

'I, and several like me have walked this planet ever since, highly specialised for one particular mission – to find and capture the *Motna* – the human who, unknown to themselves, has been appointed by the Dryads and Mankind to steal the Tangrad from its current safe place of hiding. I am simply protecting it – think of me as a grown up fairy catcher if you like, albeit a 'bad fairy' catcher.'

'You are insane.' Nathan groaned, his head bowed in anguish.

'We'll see.' Pressing a large remote control panel, Woodruff placed the room into near darkness. His voice resounded from nowhere and everywhere, echoing around the walls of the amphitheatre.

'I have to say, the fae in general, and the Dryads in particular have gotten a lot cannier about public relations with humans. The modern perception here sees them as playful, childlike, and perhaps mischievous at worst. However, all fairies possess powerful magical skills, and, when a fairy 'goes bad', they are ruthless, vicious aliens, hell bent on self-preservation and greed.'

The large projector screen activated, and a still image of a calm strip of water, surrounded by thousands of people illuminated the room.

Its calming effect caught Nathan's attention immediately. There was something strange about those faces in the crowd, but Nathan could not place what it was.

Woodruff continued the history lesson.

'Fairies exist on the very edges of mortal society. This is a literal and figurative statement Nathan. Literally speaking, they can be encountered outside the bounds of civilised spaces, like the wilderness. They are often encountered by hapless travellers whose roads take them through remote places removed from the safety of immediate civilisation. I need you to think about that whilst you watch this. There is no question you have been 'reprogrammed' by the Dryad, but I need to find out how and when, otherwise nothing will be gained by your interception.'

'How can you be so sure about all of this nonsense? Perhaps it's you that's been brainwashed,' Nathan retorted, his senses slowly returning in the presence of this lunatic.

'It would serve you well to watch this film first Nathan. It was taken yesterday in the harbour of Gestraan, five miles north from the palace of the Fairy Queen of Sidhle. The reason for the crowds is Parade Day, the largest royal event in the fairy calendar. Please watch carefully, as I will be asking detailed questions after.'

The imagery on the screen suddenly came to life. Against a backdrop of several enormous silver domed structures, the huge crowds cheered and waved tiny flags at something not yet in view. Something bothered Nathan about their appearance, but still he could not identify it. Before the celebrating masses, the water glistened cool blue, as shimmying light reflected from what looked like two pink suns in the clear blue sky. Nathan rubbed his eyes trying to make sense of what his mind was telling him so far.

'This is the bit where you need to concentrate,' Woodruff boomed above the noise of the crowds. 'You are about to see things you will not believe, but believe me, they are all true. They really happened. Concentrate Nathan, concentrate.'

As the crowds on the screen continued to cheer, the water changed. Trails of vapour rose into the air as it started to surge and boil. Moored boats at the far end of the harbour were tossed about like small toys. The hitherto jubilant crowd noticed as one, just as something very large and dark began surfacing with an audible squelching and sucking noise.

'What's that?'

'SSShhhh!' Nathan was cut off before he could say any more.

On the screen, mass panic broke out. A huge, scaly head broke the water's surface. Emerging on a long neck, it dripped with riverbed ooze and weed. Two enormous red eyes blazed at the frantic crowd.

Suddenly, the entire crowd moved together as one – vertically. In unison with the crescendo of their screaming, thousands of pairs of translucent, gossamer wings frantically beat at the back of every single bystander, silently moving them heavenwards – with one notable exception.

'At this point, I had better tell you that this creature is a dragon. A *visciay steglatt* breed at that. Very nasty fellow indeed.' Woodruff interrupted the show by pausing the picture just as things looked like they were going to turn nasty.

'Dragons are *very* clever creatures. They know that fairy defences are virtually ineffective against them, and they are only too aware that human defences are even worse. However, they live by eternal curse of limited movement. They just can't come and wreak terror whenever they feel like it. A dragon *has* to be summoned Nathan. This chap was summoned by someone yesterday, regardless of the consequences.'

With that, the picture rolled into life once more. Nathan felt his mind crumble whilst he watched the scene unfold before him.

Uniformed guards appeared on the scene, flying in from the corner of the screen, suspended in the air by the frantic beating of their wings. As they started shooting their strange handheld weapons at the monster, its fearsome gaze befell them in an instant. Whatever they were shooting, it was no match for the fearsome beast filling the screen. Without warning, it reared up on massive, armour-plated hind legs, obliterating the small winged men with one exhale of its fiery breath. A deafening roar filled the auditorium as the creature bellowed its defiance.

The scene was one of chaos and terror. Fire spewed forth as if the gates of hell themselves had opened. As the fairy crowds vainly attempted escape, they were incinerated as soon as they took flight. Resistance against such overwhelming odds was futile.

The images stopped once more.

'As much as I find these scenes the stuff of nightmares, it's the next bit that gets interesting. Please pay particular attention to the bottom right hand of the screen.' Woodruff now sounded like a schoolteacher addressing an evening detention class.

The show resumed for its conclusion. Immediately, a familiar voice cut through the cacophony of screaming and terror. 'Ah –Maan –wheela!' it boomed. The dragon stopped its attack, as if struck down by an invisible bullet. 'Ah – wen – tellaaan!' the new voice commanded, and the dragon immediately went to its haunches, as if pacified by the foreign sounding command it was receiving. And there it sat, perfectly still, placidly awaiting its master.

Amongst the carnage, images of partially burned fairies and blazing buildings filled the screen. Nathan had seen nothing like it before. But just as the edges of his sanity were stretched to their limit, what he saw next took him past the breaking point.

'Ahn – wassateen – leenat!' the dragon commander yelled. Its servant merely hunched back into the body of calming water, totally submerged again except for the enormous head.

From the bottom right hand corner, a new character in the production appeared. It was another fairy, only this one looked disproportionate to the rest. Although he flew, he was much clumsier than the others. There was a darkness and menace about the way he viewed the carnage around him – it was the broad smile of gratification that was most disturbing.

Disbelieving, Nathan saw himself on the screen. He watched himself fly unnaturally to the apex of the dragon's eye, administering the last command. 'Ash – Taan – Wonim!' he boomed, and, quietly, with minimum disruption to the water's surface, the massive head disappeared into the depths once more.

As the fires raged, all was quiet. Central to the screen, caught on camera forever, Nathan hovered menacingly above the harbour, his expression cold and dark. His murderous smile betrayed his happiness at the day's work.

As the lights snapped back on, Woodruff froze that final image on the screen for it to linger. He wanted it burned into Nathan's consciousness for all eternity.

'Two thousand good fairies perished in the attack Nathan. Now, let's start at the beginning shall we? ...'

Is This You, and If It Is, Do You Know Who You Are?

Unbelievably, I am using my last resort, and writing down what I need to say to you, as standard conversation without conflict has become impossible.

Why? You are probably asking, as your anger levels are likely to be rising right now, and your sense of unjustness bites deeper and deeper into your 'victim's mentality' psyche.

The answer is simple really. No matter how hard I have tried with you, I am finding it ever increasingly difficult to contain my resentment and ill feeling towards your abject failure to allow me to complete a sentence of dialogue in your presence without constant interruption, or having you speak over me (usually with rising levels of aggression). You really have no idea of the burning hatred I feel inside because of this, yet you never attempt to change or get help.

Anyway, the real purpose of this note is *not* to tell you just how much I hate the way you talk over me all the time – no – it's to tell you chapter and verse exactly what I have been trying to articulate for all these years. I guess subconsciously, I also know that you have no choice, other than to read this now, and, because you will be alone as you read, it will be impossible for you to shoot off.

Right then, now I have your undivided attention, let's go.

First – you are a complete nightmare. No person I have ever had the misfortune to come across in my entire life to date has ever pushed me so far into the absolute depths of mental darkness and despair as you have.

I am yet to meet anyone so self-absorbed with such feelings of self-pity. Ever. And yet, pity is your guiding point of reference that informs the very nature of your existence. Your filters on reality are so distorted, the act you pulled off in creating me was, in retrospect, worthy of the ultimate accolade for services to acting in general.

My life with you has become a perpetual cycle of self-doubt and anxiety, coupled with an emotional burden of expectation from you that even Solomon himself would never be able to fulfil. Whilst you continue to believe that you are so emotionally needy, that my ignorance causes anxiety for you, I could not disagree more. You are simply a control freak, insanely frustrated because you are unable to manipulate me to your personal self gain.

This frustration manifests itself behind closed doors as uncontrollable anger. Your face becomes an abstract of hatred every time we argue – yet you continually refuse to believe or accept this. At times, your actions verge on the psychotic, as the anger takes control. But somehow, you always find a way to justify it in your own mind. Don't forget, in the worst of your temper tantrums, you have threatened me with violence, physically assaulted me, humiliated me (remember my clothes on the driveway?), thrown things at me, and yet, you tell *me* that *I'm* the lucky one, and that the incidents are isolated and acceptable!

Personally, I think you're off your bloody rocker!

Putting aside the mental anguish and irreparable damage you have inflicted on me, (yes – **you** – so come down off your high horse of pious self-pity and carry on reading), I think you should also be aware of the practical hell you create in our lives.

You are a messy sloven, with no respect for your own or other people's property. An infuriatingly antagonizing defensive mechanism you invoke without fail is the one where you whine 'I have to get up on my own and organize everything every morning – all you have to do is get up.' Blah. Blah. Blah. Blah.

I get up so early to do my crappy, pin-money job because it brings money into the house. I never hear you complain when I give the monthly housekeeping. Does anyone else in my position have to work themselves into the ground and balance everything else like I have to? No. Even when I am up and about so early, you never ever acknowledge my existence before I set off.

Is it worth me pointing out that if any of the kids wake up distressed in the night, howling, screaming, coughing, puking or any other associated night horrors, no matter what hour, it's always muggins here who gets up and deals with it. You just lie in your bed, snoring, completely oblivious. I swear, if the four minute warning sounded during the night, you'd sleep right through it.

And another thing – what happens for 90% of the time every evening? Oh yes, that's right. You do nothing, and I cook and clean. So, I'm not really too sorry if it's such a hardship for you to get up off your backside without any help in the morning, but you more than make up for your exertions by helping me out to the merry tune of. 'I'm doing nothing and up yours if you don't like it …' every evening.

As for weekends – Jesus! I can't even *remember* the last time you got up before me on a weekend morning.

I would love to see you on your own for a week, without help from your mates. You'd be a wreck within six hours!

Sorry, but you really don't have a clue. In a way, I pity you. Your self-absorbtion isn't just destructive to those around you – you yourself must find it a complete source of paralysis. The only problem is that you think that your issues can be resolved by the words and deeds of others – classic self-delusion.

No matter how severe our disagreements, you seem to be able to forget every aspect of them within hours.

One minute you are literally screaming at me to get out of the house, and a few hours later you will pester me for a hug. Your ignorance is breathtaking.

Oh, for your information, here's some of the other bullshit you inflict on me with regularity includes:

You poke, you pry and you are nosy.

You don't like the thought of me having a life.

You act like a petulant child if you know I have a valid point.

You will screech hysterically at me one minute, and be nice as pie to anyone else the next. (False bitch.)

And finally, you've had such a charmed life, yet all you do about it is whinge.

There's so much more (don't even think about getting me onto the prickly subject of shopping for example), but for now, that's it. If you are numb from reading everything that precedes this point, then I will summarise.

Pull yourself together and sort yourself out. Close your eyes and count to ten, that may be a good start point. Hey – that would be progress!

Do I still love you? Yes.

Do I like you? Not one bit.

The choice is yours, but one final warning:

Force me out, and I'll see you in court.

Thanks.

I know I should show more respect for my mother, but it works both ways, don't you think?

P.S.

If you see dad, can you remind him to pick me up from school today? I've got Home Ec in the final period, and I want to keep my baking warm for you all to try when I get home.

Bye.

Falling Down

Even by my own standards, I have to admit my career was outstanding. By the History of which my legacy will be measured, I improved the lives of millions. *That's* how good I was.

At the height of my powers, I was *the* most famous, recognizable man walking the planet. Not too long ago, I was indeed a global icon. Unfortunately, that was in another lifetime, an eternity ago.

My heart is currently filled with sorrow, although I have much to be proud of. I would even go so far as to call myself fortunate – well, until earlier today, anyway.

You may know who I am – (who am I kidding? – of course you know who I am!) – But for those of you locked away in the broom cupboard for the last quarter of a century or so, allow me to introduce myself.

My name is Frederick Templeton Adams, forty-seventh President of the United States. I'm also the first catholic, black holder of the job, so my notoriety was assured in the history books the minute I set foot over the threshold of the West Wing.

As you will know, I was a brilliant diplomat who improved the lives of every soul in the country through sweeping tax reforms. I am a proud man, and what I am sharing with you now is because of the position I find myself in.

Virtually every citizen of earth will at this very moment be glued to their TV monitors, receiving changing updates on today's events. Every nuance of my existence has fallen under frenzied media spotlight for as long as I remember, but don't let that put you off. Because you have found me here, you have my utmost respect, and, in doing so, the right to know what really happened.

For the past eight years, I have not even been able to brush my teeth or visit the cloakroom without intrusion or debate on the brand of toothpaste I use, or, quality of toilet paper in the oval office. I have never been able to set foot in public without a massed rank of bodyguards tracing my every move, ready to sacrifice their lives in the line of duty in order to preserve mine.

However, what is yet to be discovered is that I have been warned in the past of my imminent extinction, even before today's events. My story is disturbing. The reason why I nearly never made it is simple and to the point. I was saved from death itself, not by a bodyguard flinging themselves into the path of an assassin's bullet, but by the intervention of supernatural forces.

Fate has always been kind to me throughout my existence. Many jealous others used to snide that I was born with a star above my head. I was always the guy who you could drag through dung, yet still come up smelling of roses.

My tale rewinds thirty years, whilst I was at home in a newly acquired country retreat, enjoying a welcome break from the incessant bustle and stress of senior diplomatic life. The property had been purchased in my name by a mutual benefactor to my position in Government, against the miserable backdrop of a nationwide recession.

Even in its infancy, my career was already distinguished, having included six highly productive years as governor of California. My role at the time of the first visitation was as tough as it got back then – Secretary of State. That year, I had been charged with overseeing the Government reorganization of a West European country, recently liberated from the tyrannical grip of its mad dictator.

This new house, situated outside a small fishing village on the eastern Seaboard, provided an ideal refuge for those frequent moments when I sought only tranquillity.

On my third night in residence, peace was shattered, and my life changed forever by the terrifying circumstances of the first visit.

By 4 am, I had been in bed for three hours. I suddenly found myself jolted wide awake, nauseous with unexplainable dread. Outside, in the grounds directly adjacent to my room, the terrifying noises that had awoken me continued, rising in volume and proximity. I could not believe I was alone hearing them, yet, no other sound circulated within the house.

Curious yet wary in equal measures, I jumped out of bed, reaching the French windows in one fleeting movement. Peering out, limbs trembling and heart racing, I could see the entire half-acre of trimmed lawns, bathed in the ethereal glow of moonlight. One small spot at the rear remained from immediate view, that which bordered the dense woodland, providing sanctuary from prying eyes. Tonight, the tall trees cast long black shadows across the back third of the garden. And from these shadows came the sounds that had woken me – heart-rending sobs, more animal than human.

Fumbling the aged window latch, I was taken aback when a man staggered from the shadows, fully exposed by moonlight. He was bent double under the weight of a large load on his back. At first, I thought it was a long linen chest – but, as he came closer, I could clearly see the chest was in fact a coffin.

As fast as my legs would allow, I descended the large staircase three at a time, threw open the courtyard door, ran across the lawn, shouting at the wailing man to halt. Up to this point, his face was obscured, held down and hidden by the shadows. On hearing my shouting, he lifted his head, looking straight at me.

Bright moonlight fell on a face so unforgettably loathsome – freakishly disfigured, contorted with hate and fury – I was stopped dead in my tracks.

Drawing upon my remaining reserves of courage, I decided to run at him to scare him away. As I advanced, he did not move. My momentum was such that a collision was unavoidable. I closed my eyes to brace for impact – and ran right through him!

At the same time, he disappeared into thin air – coffin and all. With his disappearance, the gloom in the atmosphere lifted around the entire house and grounds.

Returning to my bedroom trembling and puzzled, I immediately made a shaky entry in my diary, retired to bed, and tried to sleep.

During breakfast the next morning, I read my account to the staff, appealing for an explanation, but none could help. The description of my visitor matched no one in the area, past or present. There wasn't even a local ghost to blame – so the event remained an inexplicable mystery.

Over the years, the memory of that strange night remained – but failed to trouble me as time progressed. I convinced myself it was nothing more than an extraordinarily vivid nightmare. And that's how things stood for the next three decades.

Earlier today, my vision returned, taking on new significance.

My French state visit was progressing magnificently. Previous tensions between our nations long smoothed over by my own long-standing personal friendship with the French leader.

Amongst the normal melee that follows me everywhere, (but particularly here – such is my personal popularity), I was attending a diplomatic reception at the Grand Hotel in Paris.

Unsurprisingly, the foyer was jam-packed with guests who were either just waiting for a glimpse of me, or impatiently waiting for the lifts that took an age to reach the function, on this occasion being held in the presidential suite on the top floor. With my personal secretary Stella in tow, I was immediately ushered to the front of the queue. Arriving without fuss, the lift door whistled open, the attendant ushering us in.

Blood ran from my face. Stella immediately looked worried, concern etched on her face.

'Mr President?'

My heart had gone cold. My knees buckled.

'Mr President Sir?' she asked, urgently. 'You don't look well at all. I'm calling a medic.'

Before the eyes of the watching world, I froze to the spot, fighting to breathe. To the masses watching on their televisions, I was having a respiratory episode.

'No. It's OK,' I gasped, slightly disorientated.

Making no excuses, I grabbed Stella by the arm, and stepped backwards, demanding a route to the nearest concealed exit.

Naturally, my bodyguards went into overdrive, and as my health crisis was relayed in pixel perfect detail, we were ushered to a delivery bay, ambulance at the ready – something of a folly, as physically, I was perfectly fine.

Whilst I lay in the back of the ambulance, being rushed by a frantic crew to the nearest hospital, the real national crisis was unfolding back at the Grand Hotel.

As is normal protocol, despite uncertainty about my health, the reception continued. Projecting Gallic calm, the French contingent crowded into the lift – and, whilst I vainly pleaded with the paramedics I was actually fine – so it began its laboured climb.

I was being ushered into the emergency unit of the hospital when the *real* news came. There had been an accident at the hotel. A main cable in the lift shaft had snapped, sending it hurtling to destruction – within it, the French President. A massive rescue effort was under way.

For the second time in minutes, my heart froze. Guilt befell me like a thick fog. Everything was making sense now.

Lying in the relative peace and tranquillity of my private room, the outside world was clamouring for an update. I can hear the questions:

'What is the diagnosis?'

'Is his condition life threatening?'

'What stopped him from entering the lift?'

'Has he been told of the French contingent?'

And so on.

Yes, I have been told of the French contingent. The official response from my office is more than adequate:

'President Adams is undergoing extensive tests and will stay here overnight under observation. His condition is stable, and his life is not in danger. The President wishes to convey his thoughts and sympathies are with the French nation at this tragic and difficult time.'

The truth is a more startling. I am under mild sedation. Half the French cabinet perished in the accident, including their leader. He made it to hospital barely alive, succumbing to his injuries one hour ago. I have lost a good personal friend.

My mind is a little numb with the effect of the drugs, but I am crystal clear on one thing. I will never share this with *anyone*, yet its detail explains everything. It's my point of reference when I reflect on this tragic episode.

There was only one reason I did not get into that lift, and that reason must have perished with the others in that most horrible of ways.

The features were unmistakeable – he hadn't aged in thirty years. When those doors opened, and the lift attendant, with his familiar, grotesque hate-fuelled face looked back at me, thirty years of uncertainty and fear swallowed me whole.

All that was missing was the coffin.

Bat's Eye View

Everything fell apart on my birthday earlier this year.

Until then, my life was charmed. Riches, good health, security and the love of a caring, close-knit family mapped out the very fabric of my existence.

Professionally, business was booming. I had gone it alone, setting up by myself a decade ago. Following the customary hard slog of eighteen hour days, seven day weeks, fifty-two weeks a year, scrimping, saving, begging, borrowing, blagging, networking, wheeling, dealing and self-publicising – hand in hand with the obligatory fear filled sleepless nights, worrying when it was all going to go wrong, or fear of rejection by my customers – D.C Jenkins, (That's me) had become the *the* preferred supplier of 'Optimum solutions for every literary need.' In plain English, I had opened a small yet quirky bookshop in the centre of the small town where we lived, which by hard work and good fortune evolved into what was now a chain of fourteen stores across the North West of England, complete with a compact distribution centre and head office.

I need to point out right now though, this isn't a tale of 'how I made it from nothing after working my guts out' story. No, it's about what happened after that – namely the catastrophic events following the advent of my fiftieth – and pigging out on that bloody cake.

* * * * *

So, there I was on my special day, at home, enjoying a rare moment of relaxation, for once not worrying too obsessively about the business – something of a miracle really – after all, if *you* had the employment of 500 people in fifteen locations, a recent £1 million IT upgrade investment plus a logistics infrastructure that not only took in the warehouse itself, but also five self-owned delivery vehicles that needed to be kept on the road every day, (not forgetting that this little lot generated an annual turnover of £200 million – that's a lot of books), and it was all bought and paid for by *you* (well, heavily borrowed, but still being paid for by instalment to more creditors than I cared to think about), I think *you'd* be a little tense most of the time too, I'm sure.

Anyway, back to my birthday. On that particular evening, I was at home with my devoted wife, two kids and one mother. Not wishing to make a fuss, despite the milestone age reached, I requested a quiet family affair. Being such a success story in business (had I mentioned the numerous entrepreneurial awards?) made me something of a local celebrity, and, as such, going out without unwelcome intrusion – from complete strangers eager to shake my hand or talk to me about *their* money making ideas – was impossible. (Although, I also recognize these very same people are the ones that spent money in my shops, making me what I was.)

Instead, I requested we stay at home in our main residence (the two holiday homes abroad just seemed inappropriate for what was, in the main, another ordinary day), enjoy a wonderful home-cooked meal, and just be a family for once. Bliss.

Once afflicted with significant wealth, (mine came with rapid expansion caused by the surge in demand for celebrity autobiographies penned by the gossip magazine regulars), it's the simple things in life – things money can't buy – that become most important. It is a philosophy I concur with completely.

Thus, when my long-suffering mother asked what I would like as a 'special treat' for my birthday (as she had done for my entire life, just as many mums do, regardless of the age of their offspring), it was one of those simple things that popped into my mind. 'Would you bake me a birthday cake?' I asked, inspired by my childhood memories of her home-made sponges. In my early years, she had been good enough to have made a living from it.

Her face immediately lit up, overjoyed at such a personal, emotive request. After all, amongst all the trappings of success, a sense of purpose is vital for everyone involved (even if it is only to bake a cake), otherwise you can easily crack up. 'Of course!' she squealed in unabated delight, her eyes dancing with excitement, clapping her hands in anticipation. 'I'll do your favourite!'

'My favourite? Do I have one?' Whilst my memories of various concoctions were still strong in my mind, one particular delight never sprang to mind. However, it was important to recognize it must be true – we all had favourite treats as kids – didn't we?

'Oh yes! When you were much younger!'

'I can't remember!' I didn't want my lack of recall to cause her too much distress in her excitement.

'Pear and Apple Upside Down Cake! Home-made! I used to make you one every week!' Her eyes danced at the joyous memories, and, for a split second, I could almost see the image of myself as a small boy in them, loved, nurtured and spoilt rotten by an adoring mother. Yet, I was stunned that such clarity from her take on the past was not shared by myself. In a way, I felt a little ashamed I could not connect with her ecstatic recollection, and truly embarrassed that an eighty-five year old woman could summon up such memories as if they only happened an hour ago, whilst I flailed helplessly in conjuring the same images.

'You were such a little pig! Wolfed down as much as you could get your pudgy hands on! Sometimes you would refuse to eat anything else!' If there had been anyone else in the room at the time of this conversation, including the wife and kids, I would have probably seized up from acute embarrassment on the spot.

'And you almost always made yourself sick when you ate too much. Oh yes, you loved your Upside Down Cake!' There was a brief silence between us before she stood and purposefully marched across the living room towards the kitchen area. 'I'm going to start right away!' And that was that. In the week preceding the great event itself, my mother embraced the project of creating the greatest Upside Down Cake known to mankind, almost to the point of obsession – or maybe that was just simply devotion?

For the uneducated among us, (including myself), an Upside Down Cake is for real, and can be found in any recipe book containing a pudding section. Usually consisting of a combination of fresh fruit, the cake is created by placing the fruit of choice underneath a sponge mix, then baking them in extremely high temperatures for about forty five minutes. Once complete, when the cake is removed from its baking tin, the glazed front is sitting on top of the sponge layer, giving the appearance it has been baked the wrong way round – hence the name.

Therefore, it came to pass that evening; my cake was duly presented, resplendent with fifty candles and a serenade from my nearest and dearest. Strangely, my first impression was of how ugly and unappetising it looked. Nonetheless, visual representation counts for nothing if food tastes good, and this cake was absolutely delicious – like nothing I had ever tasted before – a complete, total and utter good time assault on my taste buds. My first slice was *devoured*, much to the humour of those around me. Whilst having no memory of this particular culinary childhood delight, I quickly scoffed another four slices in quick succession, to the point where my waistline became distended, which I knew would cause me even more consternation in the morning when the guilt of eating so much would consume me, not to mention the likely unsettled stomach.

Eventually, once the conversation revolving around the merits of mothers' baking (by me), and gathering old age including general ridicule about my receding hairline and expanding waist (by the kids), I retired to bed in the small hours, stomach swollen from over-indulging, breathless from carrying the extra weight up the stairs. Unexpectedly, I was also struggling to shake off a peculiar, dull thumping in the back of my head. I didn't sleep well at all.

Next morning, after an intermittent, disturbed evening of ruffled sleep, the gluttony of the night had manifested as a nasty nauseous feeling in my stomach and throat I knew would last for *hours*, and, even more bothersome, the headache remained – relentless, dull, throbbing and, by now, all consuming. Coupled with an indescribable 'out of sorts' sensation (that wasn't lethargy, but sluggishness due to overdoing the calories? – it could well have been), I hesitantly crawled into the car, aiming for the office. I was due to visit several stores later in the day with a key supplier's rep, but such were my symptoms, I called through in advance to Chris, my PA, ordering her to cancel. 'What reason shall I give?' she testily barked, 'Tell them I'm ill. We'll reschedule when I'm better.'

'Fine,' she sighed heavily, and hung up. She hated having her routine broken. She also knew that I would only cancel such a meeting in extreme circumstances, so she was likely to be concerned not just to the PR impact on the business (publishers *detest* being mucked around), but also my welfare and wellbeing.

After a challenging drive, having found it extremely difficult to concentrate due to the continual tub thumping in my head that even four of the toughest of painkillers on the market (allegedly) had yet to dent, I finally arrived. Shuffling through the main entrance, I muttered a brief greeting to Chris, telling her to hold all my calls as I didn't want to be disturbed, and shut myself in my compact, yet inviting office, immediately pulling the previous day's as yet unread financial reports to pore over.

For reasons I am still unable to explain, my usually obsessive desire to conduct a detailed examination of every line and column on the report dissolved completely as soon as I sat down before them. Suddenly, incomprehensibly, it just didn't seem important any more.

During the course of the morning, the headache diminished slightly, as did the nausea and creaking belly. Only by drinking cold water and washing down more painkillers than was good for me every two hours kept me going. All morning I had done nothing except stare blankly at my PC screen atop the large oak desk. A sense of restlessness and anticipation crept into my consciousness, yet I didn't know why. As the day progressed into late afternoon, I had yet to emerge from the sanctuary of my private workspace. After all, it was *my* office, *my* seat of power in *my* own company. *My* company. It was in that precise moment of thought; I decided it was time for a change in *my* company.

Don't ask me why. I don't know. All I can say is that a powerful, compelling urge to suddenly transform the business overcame me – no, *consumed* me that afternoon.

As a total autocrat, my rule was, and always had been, law of the company. Whilst I had a small executive board of three so called 'directors' – installed at the behest of my creditors three years ago – every decision rested with me. Rule by committee if you like, except

I was the committee, so the executive were no more than my appointed lackeys, selected by *me* to carry out *my* wishes. Resistance was futile, so no one challenged my authority – they all knew they were there because of me after all – I paid the wages, and they knew not to bite the hand that fed them.

To that end, as I started scribbling furiously in a rushed longhanded scrawl on the first scraps of paper I could get my hands on, it was in the knowledge these sudden and immediate changes would be embraced and adopted without hesitation – even if no one agreed. As the writing flowed freely, I was unsure *why* I was instigating such dramatic change, yet, such was my unexplainable compulsion – just as a writer *must* write, or a painter simply *has* to paint – I knew I just *had* to change things.

As the afternoon collapsed in pieces to the ground, allowing evening to make a brief appearance, babysitting for the onslaught of night the words – or policy changes – flowed freely, without obstacle or hindrance. With every passing minute, monumental changes were created by my own hand, affecting all of my employees – yet the thoughts and deeds of head and hand felt strangely disconnected from rest of me, as if I were there, but somehow not. Once completed, the pen mercifully rolled from the edge of the desk, scuttling across the floor, preventing me from wishing to continue. My work was completed, without the need for revision. And yet, as I reviewed the labours of my effort, the words seemed alien, distant and remote from my own perceived wisdom of what constituted common sense. These were not my instructions or policies – I was incapable of such thinking, but my determination to adopt this foreign body of words as new company policy with immediate effect was unshakeable.

Adjusting the small brass desk lamp to combat the darkness engulfing every cubic millimetre of the office, every letter, every word, sentence and paragraph seemed perfect, on one level, yet something about it felt wrong, but no urge to resist existed. My head felt occupied, torn and divorced from the real me as I re-read the whole piece in its entirety once more:

Internal memorandum

From: David Jenkins

Date: 30/11/2003

To: All Employees

Ways of Working – Philosophy Changes with Immediate Effect

Commonsense for Bats – Upside Down Thinking for All Employees

1.   Current Philosophy:

'This Organization is its people's greatest resource.'

New Philosophy:

'If you aren't a manager – take something back!'

I wish to make it perfectly clear to all staff – 'this organization' is my work of fiction, invented to achieve something that cannot be done by me alone. With immediate effect, every employee must take responsibility for using the organization's capabilities to provide for the learning and development of improved working attitudes, behaviours and conditions. It is about time management within this organization gave more back in order to improve something, anything, for those that continue to labour without recognition. Be demanding of you line manager now!

2.   Current Philosophy:

'Implement My Ideas Faster.'

New Philosophy:

'Go Slower!'

As of now, I strictly forbid the upholding of the culture that believes 'We have great ideas – we just don't implement them, we're not allowed.' Great ideas are now permitted without prejudice. Additionally, they will *all* be accepted and embraced by every level of management, provided the following criteria has been met in the construction of your idea – 'Like a fine wine, great ideas take time to mature. To fully explore and develop the characteristics of your idea, don't just do something, do nothing.'

3.   Current Philosophy:

'Listen to Customers'

New Philosophy:

'Ignore Them.'

Let's be honest, every breakthrough this Company has ever achieved in product and service offer has not come from talking to customers – they came from me. With immediate effect, all staff are forbidden in delivering customer service best practice. You decide what's best instead.

4.   Current Philosophy:

'We need to be more focused.'

New Philosophy:

'Unfocus.'

Forget focus groups, and what all other well informed people think about the here and now. Obtain you ideas for the future wellbeing of this business from strangers, mavericks, players or the competition.

5.   Current Philosophy:

'Experience is Essential.'

New Philosophy:

'Stay in your role for longer than a month and face formal performance management for failing to move with the times.'

Develop your mind as a naive beginner every day. Forget the dogma of our professional morals, be ignorant at all times.

Failure to comply with the above philosophies from immediate effect will result in commencement of disciplinary proceedings for potential gross misconduct on the grounds of deliberate failure to adhere to company policy relating to unprofessional behaviour, philosophy denial, and unreasonable refusal to comply with the wishes of your pay lord and master.

D.C Jenkins

30/11/2003

Why was I so determined to make such crazy reverse thinking a suicidal hard and fast rule? To this day, I really can't be sure – I just *knew* it had to be done.

Taking my place at the hitherto unused desktop PC, I began typing, formalising the messy notes, ready for the masses to pick up in the morning. I pounded at the keyboard into the early hours, oblivious to my surroundings, time and environment whilst my frantically racing mind kept me peculiarly vital.

I knew it was right.

I didn't trust my so called 'experts' in HR

I knew it was right.

I didn't believe in expensive consultants.

I knew I was right.

I never found a business book that actually worked.

I knew I was right.

I was bringing my business into the 21st century.

I knew I was right.

They were my ideas, my words.

I knew I was right.

Wasn't I?

Noting the wall mounted digital clock glowered at me once I had finished at 4.45 am, I leant back in the creaking leather chair, took a deep breath, closed my eyes, and pressed send. There was no turning back now. In the fraction of a second it had taken my heart to beat, the policy was now sitting in every single electronic 'in' box in the company.

That was six months ago …

Within one week, the entire executive had resigned. Store staff were reported to be telling customers 'what they really thought of them' – all of it unprintable. The customer feedback section of the stores website went into meltdown with the volume of complaints, crashing the whole thing indefinitely.

Within two weeks, stores were not opening on time, if at all, and where they did, shelves were emptying, unreplenished due to the creaking logistics infrastructure. I persevered with the new philosophy.

Within three weeks, every distribution driver had walked out, stating overly aggressive and insolent store staff meeting them during deliveries when their trucks were half empty. I persevered with the new philosophy.

Within four weeks, the distribution centre was full of hundreds of thousands of pounds worth of books, whilst the handful of stores still trading were full of empty shelves.

Within five weeks, the banks had cottoned on, and were sending strongly worded letters of concern, whilst the local media had a field day, reporting the 'Self-Inflicted Destruction of a once great brand, and regional success story.' I persevered with the new philosophy.

Within six weeks, D.C Jenkins imploded under the weight of total anarchy. The stores stood empty and ransacked, the staff long gone. I called in the receivers to clear up the mess, and viewing the wreckage from a distance, filed for bankruptcy.

Within two months, the prosecutions – corporate and private – were flooding in, court summonses were fast approaching three figures in their number, and a bulk civil claim for constructive dismissal on behalf of every single member of staff sat on my mantelpiece.

Within three months, I was ruined, broken, and destroyed – homeless, with my wife, children and mother disowning me – betrayed and utterly devastated beyond forgiveness.

During the entire sorry episode, I had shut myself away, determined to oversee the collapse to the very end, making sure nothing got in the way of obliterating everything I had built from scratch. And the really scary thing? I still don't know why. It just had to be done. No matter what.

Today, my isolation room is comfortable. My doctors think I will get better soon. They say I am unique, that they have never come across anyone quite like me before. They think I have a badly connected electrical impulse running riot in my brain, which manifests itself as an involuntary ability to think and act in reverse. It's become the dominating force in my existence. Even the specially flown in 'experts' who have been sent to examine me are baffled. All I keep hearing is them asking, 'What on earth could be the trigger for such an extremely destructive sequence of events?'

Apparently, someone as bright and successful as me should never be in this situation. Genius is always tinged with madness, yet never such an acute and extreme variant.

I don't know why either. My mother has a lot to answer for. None of this wouldn't have happened if it weren't for that bloody cake – I'm convinced of that.

Winds of Change

Soon the storms swept eastwards, the sky cleared and the sun beat brutally down on the little house by the cove; and after three sweaty uncomfortable days, the stench from the garage above them became unbearable.

The magnitude of nature's wrath had been decisive, swift and sudden. Everything about their best-laid plans had gone wrong, and they had nothing more than the great British weather to thank for it.

The plan had been simple. Tony and Francis were under strict orders. They were to travel to the Humberside address scratchily etched onto the back of the utility bill envelope.

Upon arriving, they were to gain entry into the property, but only when certain it was empty. Once access was obtained, they were to search the premises up and down, end to end, until they found what they needed.

Tucked into the back of an inconspicuous aged, battered white transit van, (despite their protestations, they had no choice in the mode of transportation), the four hundred mile journey by secondary roads was one of the most uncomfortable experiences in their lives. Eventually, they reached their required destination – where things went from bad to worse.

During the northbound journey, the weather worsened considerably. When arriving, whilst the screaming wind rocked the van, such was its strength, sea salt rain fell with tremendous force, prickling and stinging exposed flesh. Judging by the coastal horizon, its worsening was imminent.

They walked the winding path towards the front of the isolated white bricked house, shielding their features in vain against the abrasiveness of the elements.

Before even reaching it, the weather-beaten, stained oak front door was flung back with incredible force from the inside, and there, unexpectedly greeting them, was the owner and target, Jimmy Tipper.

'Who the hell are you and what do you want?' he bellowed against the increasing force of the gale. Judging by his expression, Tipper was in no mood for unexpected visitors.

So completely taken aback at his appearance, neither visitor was quick enough to think of a situation defusing response. Stuttering and stumbling for words, Tony managed stammering, garbled phrases before a mobile phone burst into life. Tipper answered it angrily. Rushing back into the house to speak, the two visitors stepped gingerly into the storm porch to shield themselves.

'I thought he was out of the country,' Francis hissed.

Above the thundering wind and crashing sea, the special agents picked snippets of conversation, and, to their highly trained ears, it seemed Jimmy was arranging a drop-off.

Without warning, a gut-wrenching tearing, followed by the clearly distinguishable sound of falling masonry, caught their attention.

Jimmy snapped his phone shut, again rushing to the front door. Turning to his visitors, hostilities temporarily forgotten, he screamed.

'Are you coming to help me or what? My house is falling down!'

Automatically, they proceed outside the property, to be met with the sight of shattered, splintered masonry spread across the garden. The chimney to the old cottage had disintegrated under the visceral force of the wind.

Jimmy screamed again, his exclamations of anger drowned by the deafening roar of sea and wind colliding cataclysmically. As the ground beneath them shook, the three men were unsure if they were stood in the epicentre of an earthquake, such was the violent collision of these titanic elements.

Francis screamed at the top of his lungs above the maelstrom. 'Get back inside, now!' His efforts met without response, as Tony stood transfixed looking out to sea, and Tipper rallied back and forth across his garden, vainly collecting the fractured remains of his chimney flue. His mouth formed and spat curse upon curse, unheard above nature's cacophony.

An apocalyptic roar smashed their collective consciousnesses. All were rooted to the spot in fear, as approaching them at unimaginable speeds, a monstrous tidal wave. A churning thrashing solid wall of water one hundred feet tall ploughed the open sea, gathering momentum with every inch swallowed in its path.

'The basement! Tipper bellowed, inaudible, yet the movement of his lips enough for the two visitors to understand. 'Follow me!'

Obediently, they followed Tipper to the side of the house, leading to a separate garage building. Weaving between two luxury sports cars, he opened a large steel trapdoor, set in the concrete floor to the rear. Despite the extremity of the situation, Tony noticed this building was a recent addition.

'Shut the door behind you!' Tipper yelled, taking the steep flight of aluminium steps to the void below. Francis was second in, immediately taken aback by the basement contents. As Tony clattered the door closed, descending the half dozen steps, Tipper took charge.

'Sit there, and don't say a word. When all this ends, you won't breathe a word to anyone about this place.'

Obeying without protest, they sat on the small wooden bench, taking in their surroundings, knowing one small misdemeanour could be fatal. Around them, three basement walls bristled with hand-held guns, rifles, grenades and missile launchers. They were stockpiled in lidless crates, intended for use, not show.

'What you staring at?' Tipper barked, menace crackling his voice.

They remained silent, assessing the situation's severity. At the south end of the large room, the wall was bare, its naked concrete accompanied by a small Formica table, and single chair. Upon the table sat a modern radio transmitter.

'Can we contact the outside world?' Tony asked; keen to ensure no possibility of isolation existed.

'Maybe, but I will decide when.' Tipper glared, suspicion returning now there was time to think.

Above them, the wave crashed ashore, frantic and thunderous. Suddenly, the lights went, plunging them into darkness as the waters above thrashed and churned their onward path of destruction.

'Now I don't know who you are, or what you want, and right now, I don't care if you're Jehovah's witnesses, double glazing salesmen or undercover cops; but you'd better realize you're in my property, and the noise we can hear is the sound of my home being torn to pieces.' Rage boiled his unseen face. 'You'd better have some good answers if we get out of this alive, otherwise I will finish you off instead,' he bellowed in the darkness, defiant, driven by rage and loss.

Francis shifted uncomfortably, grateful that the pitch black room failed to betray the anguished look on his face.

'But for now, whoever you are ...' a small lighter flame illuminated Tipper's narrow, pitted face, '... help me get the power on.'

They stood up, taking his lead as several hundred thousand pounds worth of weaponry crates were moved from the east wall, allowing access to its hidden panel, concealing the small petrol driven generator, complete with fifteen pungent five litre cans of fuel. Tipper had prepared for any eventuality.

'Previous owner had this place built at the height of the cold war. Everything's reinforced, although no one told him that the hole he dug wasn't deep enough!'

'Anyway, when I bought the place last year, I thought it would be a shame to let this go to waste, so I updated it a bit, and voila!'

Tony and Francis were extremely unsettled by Tipper's extreme change of mood – he now acted like a spoilt child showing off new toys.

'There's enough juice to last us five days. If we can't get out of here by then, all power is gone forever.' He filled the generator as he spoke.

'What about food and water?' Francis felt he knew the answer.

'Five days supply behind the wall opposite, just give me one second, we'll get powered up, and …' Phosphorous lights buzzed into life, as did the static of the radio transmitter, accompanied by the rattling drone of the generator.

'I'm sure we'll get used to it!' Tipper grinned. 'Now, we need to move some of this stuff around again ...' He arced his arms towards the crates of grenades and launchers. '... but be careful, it's fragile!'

Gingerly moving the dangerous cargo focused their minds. They carefully shifted the crates of warmongers toys as Francis' mind raced.

They knew Tipper as nothing more than a modern day pirate, cheating HM customs of thousands in duty revenues. His cloak and dagger operations bringing illegal cigarettes and alcohol from the continent were his speciality, but nothing like this. This was a weapons factory.

'What's all this for?' Francis spluttered.

'I ask the questions, not you.' Tipper barked, eyes dancing crazily. 'Remember, you're on my turf pal. Because of me, you're still alive.' He paused, adding menacingly 'Let's just say I've plenty of paying customers for this merchandise, and business is booming.'

'Bingo!' Tipper exclaimed as a green padlocked door was exposed, then unlocked, revealing row upon row of tinned food and bottled water.

'Like I said, there's enough for five days should we need it. Glad I was so thorough in my preparations.'

It was obvious that Tipper was no small time pirate. Those activities merely presented a front for the real work that went on here. Every eventuality had been planned for, including the possibility of going to ground should a deal go bad, or, the authorities got too close.

'Right then,' Tipper broke the silence once again, passing around small bottles of water. 'It's time for you both to let me know who you are and why you're here. Take your time, there's no rush.'

And so the state of tense suspicion began.

Amazingly, Tony and Francis recalled their mission scripts, kept their minds clear, delivering a convincing tale that they were actually government land prospectors, who'd identified one thousand acres of coastline 'at risk' from natural erosion.

Tipper's response betrayed his suspicions.

'So why'd you come all this way to see *me*?'

Sticking to the script, they convinced Tipper theirs was an initial scoping visit, designed to assess the risk to his property. Tippers eyes widened when Tony summed up the purpose of such activity.

'To cut to the chase, Mr Tipper, we were sent to agree the size of the financial compromise package the Government is offering. We're here to tell you of your compensation.'

'So you're not coppers then?'

'No,' Francis lied convincingly. 'We came to make you rich.'

Tipper visibly eased, though still keeping a steely grip on his shotgun.

Over the following seventy-two hours, the three men co-existed in a perpetual state of suspicion, as if replicating a hostage situation.

Conversation kept to the standard format Tipper insisted on – he asked the questions, Francis and Tony provided answers. As Tipper held a gun, Francis and Tony worked very hard at maintaining the façade.

Despite his best efforts, Tipper failed to make contact with any of his cronies using the sophisticated radio equipment. 'Piece of crap,' Tipper hissed, fighting violent instincts to throw it across the room.

They tried on the hour, every hour, working in shifts so that each of them was able to take a few hours' sleep at a time.

Unsurprisingly, when Tipper was due sleep, handcuffs incarcerated Tony and Francis further, attaching them to the base of the retractable ceiling ladder. As a precaution, they remained silent whilst Tipper slept, as a mind as suspicious as his never switched off.

On the third day, with food and water running low, and patience wearing thin, the noise above subsided.

'About time too!' Tipper screamed, more in relief than anger. He scratched at his ragged stubble growth as he spoke.

Despite his forward planning in expecting the unexpected, Jimmy Tipper failed to install any wash facilities. They all stank.

'Thank God!' Francis muttered, grateful for the opportunity to leave.

'When should we try to go?'

'Now!' Tipper barked. 'It's as quiet as a library.'

Yanking the small ladder into position, he ascended.

'Do you think it's safe? After all, a lot of damage will be up there.'

Glaring malevolently, Tipper pushed against the hatch with his shoulder. For the first time in three days, he allowed the gun out of his hands. Neither Tony nor Francis took their chance to finish the assignment, so the gun remained on the table, loaded yet untroubled.

The hatch crashed open with enormous protest. The stench assaulted their nostrils immediately.

'What happened up here?' Despite his reservation and the cloying odour, Tipper clambered through the hatch without looking back.

He groaned from beyond ceiling. 'Quick, get up here quickly, both of you. Bring the gun, we'll need it!'

Tony picked up the gun, following Francis up the small narrow aluminium steps, hauling himself into the newly formed world.

Everywhere they could see, devastation reigned supreme. The landscape was unrecognisable. Earth had been flattened. Where sturdy brick buildings once stood, all that remained were sodden piles of rubble.

The sky was dark, spinning furiously. The sea churned, swaying and bubbling as if being boiled.

Decorating the extinct buildings, ploughed earth and ruined concrete lay the riven bodies of countless sea animals, rotting and smashed by the force of expulsion from their natural habitat.

Tony gasped, betrayed by his own senses. 'It's the apocalypse, the end of the world.'

'I dunno about that,' Tipper soberly replied 'But I feel sorry for him.'

He pointed to the grim and gruesome scene one hundred yards to their left, to the spot occupied by the biggest sea beast of all. The shark remains were at least twenty feet long. More disturbing was the mutilated, rotting human corpse occupying its stomach.

'What now?' Tipper asked, uncertain the first time.

It was Tony who, after much careful consideration responded first.

'We wait to be rescued. Someone will come for us. It may take some time, but they'll come … won't they?'

Days in Paradise

No sooner had the receiver of the constantly ringing telephone been returned to its cradle, it once again shrieked throughout the cramped, confined space of the busy office. 'Not another one!' groaned special investigator Albertine Crave, shaking her head in disbelief. 'I'm not getting that one; I've already picked up three nasties today!' She folded her arms in deference to emphasise her point. The remaining occupants of the Nursery character Authority for Control Against Random Disciplinary Decisions central operations room all stared at each other pleadingly, hoping against hope that someone would pick up the call.

After twenty-four unanswered rings, the screeching telephone continued to penetrate the tense atmosphere of the NACARDD office. Whoever was trying to get through was either determined, angry, worried, fed up, feeling put upon, or just wanted to pick a fight. Or all of them.

'OK. OK!' sighed super special investigator Macey Madderly, dramatically swiping the receiver from the cradle, knocking over a half-consumed cappuccino across a stack of scattered paper work littering her large desk. Closing her eyes, she clenched her teeth tightly as she greeted the caller. 'Hello, NACARDD, how can I help you?'

Her features were eerily illuminated by the blue screensaver floating across the face of her desktop monitor as she listened intently, making careful notes whilst the caller downloaded what would be yet another tale of perceived woe and injustice. Throughout the conversation, Macey only punctuated her responses with the odd Uh … Huh, OK, or hmmmm. Only once did she have to ask for the caller to repeat themselves. This was a bad sign – the caller was calm and rational – that could only mean a trouble case.

Whilst Macey continued taking details from the anonymous caller, the NACARDD team were slowly coming to terms with the sheer volume of work sitting firmly within their jurisdiction. So many botch-ups, and so little time to deal with them.

Albertine Crave had already buried her head in an enormously thick file marked 'Lucy Locket', furiously scribbling notes and making endless references to a key data bank she had pulled up on her PC screen. That particular case was a difficult one, full of unexpected twists and turns. A badly flawed investigation coupled with a falsified witness statement from Lucy herself had led to the wrongful dismissal of Kitty Fisher on the grounds of deliberate failure to comply with the published rules of the Company relating to cash procedures. It was only with the careful forensic expert analysis of Albertine that the placement of every penny was found and placed back in the pocket with the ribbon round it. Subsequently, Kitty was reinstated and Lucy Locket was now suspended on full pay, under investigation herself for Gross Misconduct on the grounds of deliberate falsification of records. Albertine was pulling together the numbers in preparation for her statement tomorrow morning.

To her left, Inspector Flickie Noodly of the Hospital Ward Division incessantly tapped away at her keyboard, compiling a complicated financial document headed 'Incey Wincey Spider'. Now well into its thirty-second week, the Spider case had the makings of setting a dangerous precedent. The external LOD Field Operative assigned to the case had played everything by the book. Following the incident, all relevant accident report forms were duly completed, equipment tested, and safety inspections conducted. Negligence had been ruled out – Incey had simply been the innocent victim of a freakish accident.

Throughout his sickness absence, all policy and procedure had been followed, with meetings at eight and thirteen weeks of absence providing additional support to Incey and his family. Doctors' notes were handed in on time, and formal communications had been acknowledged without any resistance.

It came as quite a shock, when, following the doctor's report on the twenty-sixth week of absence, and Incey's subsequent dismissal on the grounds of ill health, the decision to dismiss was formally appealed. In his letter of appeal, Incey claimed that he had irrefutable proof that the garden water spout had indeed developed a dangerous fault, additionally deeming his dismissal unfair due to the fact eight broken legs take significantly longer to heal than two. The case was about to go to a final independent appeal, yet, with the cloud of an ET1 application hanging over it regardless. As a result of this, Flickie was working a proposal for a compromise award to settle before Incey could take proceedings further. The final decision was laced with risk either way.

'Sorry everyone.' Macey Madderly had finished the call, and looked completely drained as a result. 'But I really can't take any more on now. That was the fourteenth request for contractual information relating to an appeal today.'

'OK Mace … was it a bad one? Helly Penpaw smiled reassuringly at the Super Special. Being one of the two of LalaLand plc's RDD appointed experts, specialising in all things of a debilitating nature, Helly had a vested input and interest in every case that came into the office. She also had a sixth sense as to how those around her were coping with the record breaking number of claims circulating around them at the moment.

'Not really …' Macy hesitated. 'It was the dish and the spoon. They're definitely going ahead with their grievance.'

'Remind me again?' Helly asked, keen for any fresh angle. It was the first time a multiple grievance had come in for some years.

'They are requesting a hearing with their designated LOD Field Op as they have been unable to resolve their concerns with their line managers, the cow and the moon. They say the cat and the fiddle have been acting inappropriately at work, and it's got to a point where something needs to be done.'

'OK. Sounds fairly routine to me. So many similar ones are coming in right now – only an hour ago Little Miss Muffett called, asking for a hearing to discuss a harassment allegation against the spider that came along and sat down beside her ...' Helly paused, carefully selecting her words.

'Could you pull together all similarly themed cases of the last four weeks into a one page summary document? I'm keen to explore any potential risk of process failure by their line managers.'

'Will do. No worries!' Macey beamed, as Helly turned back to face her own pressing, unique commitments.

Old Mother Hubbard was going to tribunal under the Age discrimination act, claiming that the terming of her as 'Old' had caused her much distress and humiliation at work; she had no other alternative than to resign and claim constructive dismissal. To compound Helly's workload, The Old Woman who lived in a Shoe, inspired by Mother Hubbard, had filed a similar claim, citing discrimination from her line manager on the grounds of age and failing to observe working time regulations. Apparently, due to child care commitments as a result of having so many children she didn't know what to do, her request to opt out of working Sundays was denied without the application of the appropriate consultation process.

All hell was breaking loose with the workforce in LaLa Land plc, and as the last line of defence, the elite members of NACARDD were beginning to feel the strain.

* * * * *

As the hustle and bustle of fingers clattering keyboards and arguing about answering the telephone continued, MoeLa Raeking sat, absently staring at the illuminated screen before her. As the founder member and leader of NACARDD, hers was the greatest burden to carry. It had not always been like this.

The employees of LaLa Land plc had a reputation for being somewhat highly strung and dysfunctional, but that's what made them special, well loved and lucrative to their employers. However, with the advent of console based computer entertainment, LaLa Land's once iron grip on the children's entertainment market had been eroded considerably, and now, the Company had placed cost savings and efficiency as the prime levers to maintain profit growth. As a result, the Company's once envious reputation for looking after its characters had taken a battering in recent times.

And then came the Knave of Hearts ...

A dynamic professional, specialising in everything that can and will go wrong, MoeLa had built a team around her equipped for anything and everything. However, the Knave of Hearts controversy a year ago had changed everything. It had only seemed like yesterday.

He had been accused of stealing the tarts of his mother, The Queen of Hearts whilst they were still cooling from the oven. Suspended pending a detailed investigation; the Knave always maintained his innocence. The LOD Field Operative designated to the case had been thorough, yet very inexperienced. Based on the allegations made during the investigative interview process, disciplinary action was deemed necessary. The subsequent disciplinary interview was handled badly by the inexperienced, nervous field operative. Despite circumstances and evidence to suggest mitigating circumstances to the Knave's case, he was dismissed for theft.

Unknown to anyone at the time, the Knave had secured legal representation, and, allowing the appeals process to take due course without a reinstatement, the Knave successfully prosecuted on the grounds of non compliance to set out policies and procedures relating to the Company's discipline and grievance manual. To avoid adverse publicity, LaLaLand plc had settled out of court. To keep the Knave's silence had proved to be very costly.

Internally, the embarrassment had been immense. Much to MoeLa's disgust, not once had any of her team been consulted. Had this happened, no one would have got into the mess in the first place. For the ensuing weeks, the Field Operatives spent too much time focusing on who to blame (besides themselves) for their actions.

Meanwhile, word of the Knave's successful groundbreaking case was spreading like wildfire. The floodgates had opened. As the first line of defence, the Field Ops were OK, yet made too many mistakes. Despite being affiliated to the NACARDD department, they were controlled by another division – the LaLaLand Operations Directive, LOD for short (privately they were referred to as Legion Of Doom)– and as such, were inexperienced at dealing with such complex and critical cases. MoeLa and her team of NACARDD experts were now the 'cleaners' who sorted out the ever-increasing amounts of mess left by failings of the LOD team.

Things had changed so much. Even their offices had been downgraded and moved from a multipurpose, fully functioning, adequately equipped workspace, to their current broom cupboard out of sight and out of mind of every other head office function in the organization. Oh how the times had indeed changed.

* * * * *

'Will someone please answer that bloody phone!' MoeLa pleaded, shaken out of her reminisce by the piercing trill.

'It's your turn boss,' Flickie reminded her. 'We've all gone beyond the recommended volume of cases already.'

MoeLa had to act quickly, as she too was at breaking point. The prelim hearings in the Baa Baa Black Sheep case were due in a fortnight, and there was still an insane amount of prepping of the witnesses to do. The initial resistance statements were strong, but there would be an intense amount of cross examining once their witnesses took the stand. Everything needed to be word perfect on the day.

It was a nasty situation, with the moral reputation of the Company riding on the outcome. Baa Baa had raised a claim of racial and sexual discrimination against LaLaLand.

Unsuccessful in his application to become Mary's little lamb, he felt the decision could have been influenced by both Yes Sir Yes Sir and Mary when he heard that Mary's little lamb had a fleece as white as snow, and was a girl just for good measure.

Add to that, sixteen legislative and policy changes that needed forcing through by the end of the year, including the working time directive for all non animal or human characters, it was clear that potential meltdown was upon them.

'Unplug it for now!' Her words were calm, yet firm. Spoken like a true leader. Four pairs of eyebrows rose in unison at the request, yet Flickie took great pleasure in yanking the small three pin jack from its wall socket. Simultaneously, the team breathed a sigh of relief, even though such a craven action would be frowned upon by the unions that so closely monitored their actions.

The silence was met with sighs of relief all round.

'Right everyone, listen to me ...' She stood up, grabbing a black marker pen as she approached the office drop board. Flicking to a blank sheet, she turned to face her team.

'Each one of you, I want to record each case you currently have. We are at the point of no return, and I am going to ask for help to deal with the amount we have got on, but I can't do that without absolute clarity of every case we have on the go right now. Understand?' Helly, Albertine, Macey and Flickie nodded in unison.

'OK, who wants to go first?'

Over the next hour, every outstanding case was placed onto the drop board sheets. Their complexities were breathtaking. Enough data on each case was captured on enough sheets of paper to decorate every office wall. In addition to the day's newly opened cases, many others were at various stages of the process, such as:

The Three Blind Mice were making a claim under the DDR act, alleging inadequate provision was made at their place of work to accommodate their visual impairedness, thus presenting the opportunity to the butcher's wife to cut off their tails with a carving knife. In a separate criminal prosecution, they were claiming loss of earnings from the butcher as a result of the further disabilities inflicted upon them by his wife.

Suki was appealing a final written warning for serious misconduct for taking the kettle off again when Polly had put the kettle on in the first place. At the moment, the process was looking flawed as no statement of complaint had ever been shared with her.

Jack and Jill were refusing to answer their thirteen week sickness letters and all other attempts at correspondence following Jack's breaking of his crown on the hill and Jill's unforeseen tumbling after.

Mary Mary quite contrary had raised a grievance against her line manager claiming her character was being undermined under the terms and conditions of the mental health act. The investigation had hit a snag as her manager had now gone off sick with stress, and there was a suspicion that her staff files were not up to date.

Little Bo-Peep was due to be interviewed under the employment of young persons act. Her lost sheep had anonymously called in claiming that she had lied about her age on her application form, yet somehow it had not been picked up in the referencing process. Luckily, should the allegations be founded following investigation, she was still working her terms and conditions under a thirteen week probation period.

Jack Spratt had suspended his own wife for tampering with the fat. In response, she had made very serious allegations regarding the lean, which if proven, could constitute gross misconduct for deliberately tampering with products rendering them unfit for public consumption.

Wee Willie Winkie had been causing a storm following his suspension for deliberate failure to adhere to the Company's strict uniform policy. Despite being told that coming in to work in his nightgown was not company policy as per his staff handbook, when asked to leave the premises, he had run through the town shouting through every letterbox and banging every other window. He was now looking at gross misconduct for bringing the Company into disrepute.

Humpty Dumpty had made a personal injury claim as a result of falling from a defective wall. As things stood right now, the Company were at fault as they could not provide adequate inspection records. An out of court settlement was imminent.

Finally, the mouse of Dickory Dock was refusing to work with the clock following a sudden attack of vertigo. The manager wanted to go for a suspension to investigate for potential gross misconduct on the grounds of deliberate failure to carry out reasonable instructions from a superior. An answer was imminent following the recent referral to the Occupational Health department, who, having confirmed the case, were meeting the mouse for a private consultation next week.

'That's plenty to be going on with for now!' MoeLa grinned. 'I think we have a case for requesting support!'

'Shall we turn the phone back on now?' Macey was already reaching for the plug.

'Yes, and I'll even answer it when it rings!'

'Who are you going to ask for?' Albertine quizzed, curious as to who was out there who would be willing to come in and join the clean-up team.

MoeLa did not hesitate in her response as she reached for the newly plugged in ringing phone. 'Rhames Pillett. He's the only LOD Op out there with his head partially screwed on the right way.'

The others grinned as MoeLa took the call. Rhames would be a good addition, but he came with a dangerous reputation as being an out and out operator. Coming on board would be a whole new bag of badgers for him. It was a gamble, but one worth taking.

'Uh Huh … Hmmmm … OK … Yep … Uh Huh … OK, Bye.'

'Another bad one?' Flicky seemed concerned at the blank look in MoeLa's face following the call.

MoeLa sighed. 'There's been a violent incident between two characters in a public area. Little Boy Blue has been arrested for assault. Details are sketchy, but the LOD Ops guy who just called reckons that Peter Peter pumpkin eater is in a bad way, and that Little Boy Blue's horn may need to be surgically removed ...'

Not for the first time, a collective groan escaped their lips. As MoeLa walked out of the room to the Divisional Director's office to formally request additional manpower, she was sure that she heard one of her team refer to events as, 'Just another crazy week in paradise ...'

Quite.

Brotherly Love

Shock hit her hard as she saw him. Time had etched deep grooves in his face, and his black hair had turned grey, but it was definitely him. One word burned in her mind with unbridled intensity – revenge.

'Can you confirm it's him?' the policeman whispered as they watched the forlorn, agitated figure through the one-way mirror.

'Oh, yes, *definitely*,' Monica spoke through gritted teeth, eyes unblinking, staring disbelievingly at the detainee.

'He seems to be struggling with the lights in there – is he OK?' Despite her revulsion towards the man, concern pierced her heart as he frantically paced the room on his hands and knees, blinking furiously, shielding his eyes from the glare of the sodium bulbs above.

Without command, the young officer flicked the switch to his left, plunging the cell back into darkness.

'Are you really sure?' the policeman probed, a degree of urgency in his voice. 'It's been twenty years now, this must be a shock to you. Things must've changed.'

'Everything *has* changed,' Monica whispered, as the first tears of realization rolled down her cheeks. Inside the cell, the captive settled immediately darkness fell; he now sat rigidly in the far corner, quiet and unmoving.

'When the lights are out, he sits for hours without moving. He doesn't pace the floor, nor does he sleep. He doesn't appear to get uncomfortable, and, as you've just seen, he prefers darkness ...' The young PC hesitated, and then finished the sentence '... although he moves with the agility of a cat when he eventually gets going.'

The police contacted her three days ago, informing her of his reappearance. She had been in Australia at the time, yet, this was so important, she dropped everything in Sydney, flying home immediately.

'Tell me how you found him again, please,' Monica croaked, tears falling uncontrollably, cascading down her features in tributaries of grief.

'Are you sure? I've already ...'

'I know you have!' she hissed, afraid her voice may carry through the thick glass and concrete separating her from a person that represented everything she wanted to forget from her turbulent past. 'I want to hear it again, now I'm with him.'

Begrudgingly, the constable replayed information Monica already knew. He repeated the man was discovered three days earlier – May Day Bank Holiday – unsteadily wandering alone in the crowded city centre, barefoot, dressed in tatty frayed clothes moaning to himself, oblivious to his surroundings. He paused for breath, and then continued the verbal recall.

'Despite the chaos of the annual carnival, which had been in full swing for three hours, a bystander was concerned enough to think the distressed stranger may be ill, and approached him offering assistance …'

Monica knew what came next, bracing herself for the conclusion of the discovery of this man, who had caused so much heartache and despair, taking her to the brink of self destruction.

'His response was unintelligible, but he was carrying the envelope now in your hand. Officers were requested to assist, where he was brought into our custody. Upon opening the envelope, you were contacted immediately.'

With disbelieving eyes, Monica unfurled the scrunched envelope, reading its simple message – Monica Carter, 07963 268794 – written in the messy scrawl of a young child.

She was unprepared for this. Despite having three days to digest the news and adjust to it accordingly, the shock gripped her like a vice. This man had robbed her of everything without having the remotest thought for the repercussions of his actions. Because of him, she had been living in a prison of misery for twenty years.

An older, more senior officer walked in clutching an official document. He did not bother to introduce himself. 'The DNA match is positive.'

With those words, as the need for revenge festered intensely, compassion seeped into her thoughts for the first time.

Following his sudden disappearance two decades ago, Monica's twin brother Lance had never been heard of again. He cleared the bank accounts of their parents and left, his final legacy being a hate-filled letter complaining of his need to 'divorce' himself from his 'wretched' family.

The shock and ensuing worry claimed their mother first, twelve months following his departure. Their father had died, lost and broken-hearted, three weeks later, leaving Monica alone and isolated at the age of twelve.

Looking through the thick sheet of glass, she could just see Lance's outline through the darkness, whilst he continued sitting in the corner, still and silent. There would be time for answers later.

Enemy Friend

With its black fearless eyes full of savage, menacing intent, the creature stood its ground, unwilling to sacrifice an inch. Hunched menacingly, it was poised to launch a counter-attack within the blinking of an eye. It had been a very, very long time since it had come across such an equally determined foe – an aggressor who seemed to know no limits within their intimate pitched battle.

A low guttural snarl rumbled from deep inside its throat, escaping from pulled back lips exposing rows of severe, yet gleaming ivory, needle sharp fangs. Bristles pricked every nerve ending along the length of its spine, indicating further malevolence towards its adversary.

'Steady now sunshine …' the man whispered to it. 'You're more value to me alive.'

A sliver of blood – its own blood – trickled from the open wound behind its ear, directly into the creature's eye. A new sensation penetrated its consciousness for the first time. Pain. Discomfort. A lack of complete control. The creature had never known such strange intrusions within its existence before, and now, fully carrying them for the first time, it knew such feelings were unpleasant.

'Don't make me have to kill you …'

The man unwisely took one step forward, gravel crunching beneath his feet as he did so.

Despite the numbing sensation of pain, the creature was fuelled with a controlled rage and hatred towards this enemy, this source of threat to its existence. Despite the indecipherable noises emanating from an orifice on what the creature assumed was its opponent's head, within its own mind, the creature knew this would be a fight to the death, A duel to uphold its previously uninterrupted existence.

'I really don't want to have to kill you … I really don't.'

The man, dressed in Kevlar body armour, steel chain hand gloves and reinforced steel lined boots, took two further paces forward. His unusual attire indicated a high degree of preparation for this confrontation, even to the point of protecting his face and head with reinforced steel visor and carbon crash helmet.

Valiantly refusing to move, the creature signalled a final warning. Baring its razor sharp teeth, it suddenly rose to its haunches.

Standing at full height, its eyes fell into the direct line of sight of its aggressor.

The man paused, lost for words, assessing the seriousness of this new development. This was an unexpected move. Despite all the preparation, and the entire catalogue of scenarios played out back at base, it was not anticipated that the creature had developed the acumen – physical and mental – to be able to stand like this. Things had suddenly gone critical, and despite his orders, he would have no option but to slay the creature should it attack.

Screaming, tortured, guttural howling shattered the atmosphere, ripping through the silent air, obliterating any sense of calm that remained within the ever-expanding crowd watching the drama unfold between their eyes. Before them, the heavily armoured man had suddenly adopted a defensive stance, falling to one knee, removing the weapon from a side holster and priming it, ready to fire without hesitation.

Sensing its opponent's sudden lapse in confidence, the creature knew it had opened up a route to escape from this situation. Blood steadily flowed into its eye, partial blindness disorientating it from reality. The earlier, telling blow had been sudden and unexpected. Attacking in its usual manner, this adversary had been prepared, countering whilst the creature was in mid-flight, using a vicious, black metal cane to hook it straight to the hard gravel coated concrete in one swift movement.

The man, watched by a crowd approaching three hundred people, including two television crews reporting events live to an enraptured nation, pulled the trigger lock, simultaneously releasing the safety catch. As desperate as he was to avoid terminating this particular specimen, he knew it was now too dangerous to allow it to live. This particular breed was thought to have been rendered extinct in the great purges of ten years ago when they were deemed unsafe to cohabit with mankind. Following a nationwide spate of savage, unprovoked, fatally indiscriminate attacks, the government of the day took decisive action, and the purges freed the public of the escalating, terrifying menace. This was the first reported interception of one since those dark days. Where had it come from?

There were simply too many people around the scene now. Critical mass had been breached. It was too dangerous for all of them. Were there others?

With a heavy heart, the man cocked and aimed the laser assisted handgun.

Sensing its opportunity, the creature struck. It knew it could not defeat this wily and dangerous nemesis, but it did know that escape and freedom were a certainty. It would jump its opponent, and escape under the cover of the others of a similar kind that occupied every corner of its peripheral vision. It was time.

With the speed of a heartbeat, it launched itself towards the man, heading for a trajectory slightly above his left shoulder, howling defiance as its journey through the air commenced.

In the microsecond it too for the laser guided bullet to noisily escape from its chamber with a deafening thunderclap, its deadly trajectory impacted on its target. The fleeing creature had already reached the shoulder of the police marksman.

Lifelessly falling to the ground with a forlorn yelp and loud yet dull thud, with wild cheers of the crowd filling the distant evening, the exterminated dog lay broken and still, relieved of the torture and anguish of being the last of its type known alive on the planet. With its assassination, the job was complete. The history books would record the valiant efforts of the lone marksman who brought the final conclusion to an entire species – a species that only a decade earlier was constantly referred to as man's best friend.

Cage of Freedom

'I don't believe that children before puberty are ever clinically depressed,' the doctor responded flatly.

For Garry Cohen, this was not the answer he sought. Sitting in the cramped, busy office of world-renowned child psychiatrist, Helen Beale, the room began gently swaying as he adjusted to the enormity of what had just been put to him.

'How can you be so sure?' he whispered, hoping to provoke further debate from the petite figure with the huge reputation who was now shuffling through a two foot tall stack of papers precariously tottering on the edge of her small desk.

Sighing, more out of sympathy than anything else towards the agitated school teacher, she slowly, deliberately repeated her rationale regarding the thorny and controversial subject of child depression. 'Garry, I understand your concern, but believe me, after thirty years in the field, my experience dictates that children with emotional problems should never be treated with anything more than talk therapy attended by close involvement from the patient's family …' she paused before finishing, '… for me, the idea of a depressed child would be something completely new. They are just sad. Treating young children with chemically altering medication such as Ritalin or Prozac is nothing short of monstrous.'

'How? Why can you be so certain? What do you scientifically have that could form the basis of such a judgemental statement, doctor?'

The alarm bells had started ringing a week ahead of the new school year, when reviewing the files of his new intake tutor group. The boy, from a solid, well cared for middle-class background, had no evidence of bullying in his school life so far, and was a clearly gifted academic, even at this early age in life. Yet his file contained information relating to 'special circumstances and safeguards' that would need to be taken into account upon joining his new class. Whilst the details were vague, a small typewritten note on letter headed paper pertaining to come from the offices of the boy's GP insisted on Garry, with the head teacher or a member of the school board of governors contact him to discuss the matter further 'without prejudice, within the parameters of the patient – doctor confidentiality agreement.'

Standing from behind the desk, Helen moved around and perched herself on the front, staring Garry directly in the eye. Her green eyes blazed, yet her words came without emotion, unflinching and dispassionate in equal measures. 'The gap between a fully developed adult and an eleven year old is huge in brain developmental terms. I can direct you to an infinite amount of sources from abroad where young kids *are* unforgivingly prescribed this stuff – and the prognosis is horrendous …'

Taking the small typewritten note to the head teacher, Garry was unsurprised at the lack of interest shown in the curious doctor's letter. Despite the endless breaches in protocol and confidentiality that had led to the letter even appearing in the boy's file, his direct line report was reluctant to get personally involved.

'If you're so worried, call the bloody number,' he had dismissively grumbled from the depths of his ever-increasing workload. As with all head teachers, theirs was an existence of continual enforced measurement and observation. The fear of having a school perceived as an academic failure, and the stigma it carried, was the greatest governance of all now. Subsequently, that was all that mattered.

Compelled to explore further, and taking the response from his head teacher as a form of permission, Garry made the call which would ultimately change his life forever.

'Please, continue,' Garry urged, keen to keep her talking now she had ever so slightly opened up on the subject.

'Where shall I start?' She stood once more, pacing the small room from side to side, erasing another handful of strands from the dust grey threadbare carpet.

'Anywhere you like.'

'Officially – even though many in my profession refuse to recognize these statistics, there are an estimated 1 in 200 children suffering from clinical depression. Of these, only a tiny minority, so *specifically* affected, that antidepressants have been deemed an effective answer.' She paused, stopping in her tracks, considering her next words carefully. 'Within these minority cases, there are many documented issues of potential addiction and risks of suicide, as yet unexplored in children due to a lack of longitudinal studies. In most cases, the children prescribed Ritalin or Prozac developed symptoms of confusion, manipulation and paranoia.' Returning to the desk, her eyes pinned Garry once more.

'Ultimately, these poor kids have become labelled as institutional failures – by their own families. It's tragic.'

* * * * *

Her words hung in the air, like an unwelcome and intrusive fog of acrid cigarette smoke. 'Thanks,' Garry mumbled, placing his mind back to the telephone call three weeks previously, and his conversation with the man who claimed to be the Dr Moore of the curious letter contained in the child's entry file. Despite the distance and invisibility between them, the doctor's dialogue had an air of authority, and Garry felt compelled to listen and take action.

'He is clinically depressed, paralysed under the burgeoning pressure to succeed at school and meet the expectations of his parents. He is currently undergoing an extensive programme of 'corrective' treatment using prescribed antidepressants.'

Garry had initially been staggered by Dr Moore's justification statement. 'But aren't all kids these days?' he had retorted, beginning to wonder if some sort of sick joke were being played on him. 'The poor kid is on mind altering drugs? What's wrong with you?'

Flatly responding, the man at the other end of the phone took control of the conversation.

'I am sure you will agree Mr Cohen, children in this country are the most frequently tested schoolchildren in the world, and pupils who do not do well in national tests are increasingly seen as a threat to the development and survival of schools and the careers of individual teachers.' Garry could not disagree, but was unable to make the connection between this statement of the obvious and a request for 'special circumstances and safeguards' for one of his own, as yet unmet pupils.

'You will probably notice that he is incredibly gifted academically. As part of his ongoing treatment, his neurophysiologic state has been continually measured. I know some of what I say may sound confusing ...'

'Don't patronise me, just get on with it,' Garry snapped.

'By the time he was three, the number of natural connector points, known as synapses, in his brain reached its peak at about 15,000 in each cell last year. This is several thousand more than in a fully developed adult brain. Simply put Mr Cohen, the structure of his brain is so much more complex than the average human being, his propensity for sudden and extreme mood swings is immense.'

'So you're saying that because this kid had a big brain, it stores a heightened state of emotion – which has been interpreted as depression.' Garry seemed happy with his simplification of the point, until the doctor's haughty response levelled his thinking once more.

'Not quite Mr Cohen … This eleven year old boy has brain molecule intensity four times that of a fully grown adult. There is a direct link between the state of our brain molecules and our moods – that's a scientific fact.'

'And your point is?' Garry was becoming agitated at the pitch, pace and tone of this conversation, and more importantly, felt it was not addressing the issue of the note in the file. He still had no idea why it had been sent, or what he should be doing about it.

'It's simple Mr Cohen. Behind every crooked thought, there lies a crooked molecule. Behind every crooked molecule, lies a chemical imbalance, and with each chemical imbalance therein lie the classic symptoms of depression.'

'So what is the point of this conversation doctor? I am a simple school teacher who only wants to do what is right by his kids. How can you tell me all of this anyway? Are you really a doctor? Are you …' Tersely, he was cut off with the suddenness of his initial question being answered.

'Last week, he attempted to take the life of a close family relative whilst under the full spell of a delusional episode.'

A raging, swirling thunderstorm erupted within the confines of Garry's skull. A cacophony of simultaneous fear, anger and confusion smashed into his sense of reality. 'WHAT?' he bellowed. 'Who are you? Why are we having this conversation? Why is this child not receiving the correct care from social services? Why have we not been informed by the police? Why ...' He could think of nothing else to say.

'Mr Cohen. Let's just say the boy has very unique, high profile, powerful parents in the mechanism of the local education authority, who wish to maintain a veneer of normality. I am able to give you ample verification – I know that you personally have the senior government inspection officer attending many of your classes next week ...' Garry took a sharp intake of breath, alarmed immediately; this stranger clearly had access to sensitive, confidential school information. There was no time to ask the question, as Dr Moore continued. 'Let's just say that he has motives that stretch beyond the remits of his role, and wishes to also inspect the welfare and wellbeing of his only son.' There was no mistaking the sudden numbing of his senses. Garry was well and truly tangled up in something sinister and deceptive. He was trapped.

'He is fully aware we are having this conversation. The purpose of us speaking is simply to raise your awareness in advance of the start of term next week. I merely talk of special circumstances and safeguards in the context of your awareness of the situation.'

His heart felt leaden as Garry asked one final question. 'Are any of the other children in danger from him?'

'Only if you allow it Mr Cohen ...' There was an audible click as the line went dead.

* * * * *

'So what do I do now doctor?' Outside, a chink of sunlight had broken through the milky grey clouds, penetrating the small window of the office, offering hope as a shimmering patch of blue sky announced itself to an unassuming world.

Helen flicked back her raven hair, allowing the gentle rays of sunlight to caress her weary face. 'Tell the truth.'

'I already am. Do you think I have been led astray by the as yet undetected Dr Moore?'

She sat in the vacant chair next to him and took his hand. 'Whoever this doctor was, he knew what he was talking about. The boy has been taking Fluoxetine for twelve months. It's a very powerful compound designed to combat low activity of a natural brain chemical called serotonin – a condition associated with adult depression and obsessive compulsive disorders.' She shuffled slightly, tightening her grip of his hand as she spoke.

'Questions have been raised though, as to whether an adult, let alone a child, with paranoid fantasies gains an impetus as a result of this particular drug to fulfil a dark, sometimes murderous fantasy rather than to control that impulse.'

'Are you picking this up gentlemen?' Garry nodded towards the two dark figures lurking at the back of the office, silent, impassionate yet sinister and consuming by their very presence. Still ignoring them, Helen continued:

'For the benefit of *everyone* in the room, I believe we are facing a future in which children's mental health and wellbeing will be wrongly medicated, as parents, teachers and doctors turn to ready chemical fixes as a substitute for tackling normal childhood problems through relationships and talk therapy. It's equally worrying that it's the more affluent that will turn to the medication fix – as in this case.'

The two men moved in closer, clearly hanging on to the female doctor's every word, painstakingly recording every syllable. Clearing her throat she continued.

'Depression in children, if that is what it *really* is, is not only a consequence of family dysfunction, marriage break-ups, child abuse or combinations of genetic and environmental disadvantage. Sadness lurks in the minds of 'normal' children whose parents deliver them to £5000 a term private schools in top of the range luxury cars. Psychological childhood misery can be found in a lack of interest and interaction by negligent yet busy parents ...'

Gripping Garry by each arm, they raised him to his feet, ready to lead him to the waiting car outside.

'I'm not finished yet! Keep your hidden recording devices running!' she snapped as she took a deep breath before continuing.

'When these children falter and fail, their only means of escaping their prisons of misery and cages of sorrow will be to turn to forms of self-hatred and self-harm, informing the world around them of a need to escape to their own mental freedom. The only thing is, will it awaken over-anxious parents to their own failings and inadequacies? Will they be able to allow their children to be average or below average, allowing them time to discover by themselves who they rally are? If this is an example to go by ...' she waved her hand around the crowded office, 'then obviously not. Denial and blame will continue to dominate the very fabric of society we hold so precious.'

No one moved whilst silence crackled through the air, stoking heartfelt raw emotion.

'Thank you doctor. I'm very grateful for your input.' Garry had brought the intensity of the conversation to a conclusion. 'OK gentlemen, I'm ready now.'

As the two policemen took each of Garry's shackled arms by the elbow, leading him to the exit and waiting car outside, he turned once more to the doctor.

'I know it doesn't excuse what I did, but will I see you in court?'

'Of course, Garry. Of course.' She closed her eyes, determined not to betray her emotions by allowing tears to escape. He had been her patient for so long now, ever since he himself was just a small child, the first one to take the very medication she now derided as heresy. Except back then, she felt there was no alternative. Twenty years later, Garry was still in therapy for one of the darkest cases of intense depression she had ever come across.

She glanced at the crumpled newspaper strewn across her desk, once again reading the headline that had shaken the entire community.

'TEACHER ATTACKS SCHOOL INSPECTOR' it screamed. Within the confines of the pages, every detail of the incident in Garry's packed classroom was spelt out for the world to read.

Under indescribable life and work pressure himself, having come in for stern criticism of his teaching methods in the previous two inspections, Garry had suddenly snapped in a packed classroom, raced to the back, attacking the defenceless senior school's inspector, stabbing him in the eye with a sharpened pencil, before a group of eleven year olds, including the official's son.

In subsequent police interviews, Garry would talk of his conversation with Dr

Moore, and how it had provided him with the inspiration and justification to carry out his unprovoked attack. To date, the mysterious 'family doctor' had yet to be found, his very existence shrouded in mystery and uncertainty.

Helen stared blindly at the newspaper, tears stinging her eyes, blurring her lines of vision. Even with the passing of the days, months and years, the darkness always remained. Despite all that had gone before him, Garry had failed to escape his prison. The cage would now remain closed for the rest of his days. Such a waste. The shame. The shame. The shame.

Florence

I never really hated dad for leaving home. I just think he's been really stupid, and, judging by how sad he looks sometimes, I think he knows it too.

It's been three years now, and lots has happened since he stopped living with us.

There are some real plusses to having a split-up mum and dad, especially at birthdays and Christmas! I and Robert, my younger brother, don't complain about getting two lots of presents! The other really good thing, (most of the time), is that when we see dad now, he actually spends his time on us, which is brilliant, yet something he never did before when we were all together. In fact, mum was always nagging him to do stuff with us *most* of the time.

My name is Florence and I'm eleven years old. I was eight and Robert six when mum sat us down one dark Sunday night. She was very upset; I could tell she had been crying loads. She sat us on her bed, held our hands, and told us we had to be brave, but mummy and daddy had split up, and daddy did not live in the house any more.

I was OK with the news, as we hardly saw him anyway – he was always busy working – and when he did come home, he was always tired, grumpy and shouted lots. He worked most weekends, so we never really saw him, even when we weren't at school.

Robert was more upset, as he *really* loves dad, and thought dad was his best friend in the whole world. 'Who will play with me now?' he sniffed. He never cried or anything, but mum burst into tears.

Dad called us later that night, crying too. He kept sobbing that he loved me very much. It was all a bit daft really, I mean, if mum and dad were so upset at splitting up, why did he not just come home? When I asked him, he cried even more.

After that night, we had to wait a whole week to see dad. That *was* a long time, especially as mum still cried every day. Nan came to stay with us for that week to help mum out.

When dad came next Sunday morning, he looked so happy to see us! Robert ran out of the house and wouldn't let go of him! We went to see our other nanny with dad. He was staying with her now, and he showed us his bedroom. Pictures of me and Robert were all over the room! In the afternoon, we went to the funfair. I asked him some questions about splitting up, but I really wanted to know if he found it weird living with nanny.

At 6 pm we went back to mum. Robert and dad were really sad. I was OK, but could not work out why dad insisted on staying away from us. It made everyone unhappy.

We saw dad like this for months. It was weird, once a week is not much time. The excitement before we saw him was good, but the day went *so* quickly, we were back at mum's in no time.

I think mum hoped he would return to us after a few weeks, but when our first Christmas without him home passed by, we realized he was gone for good.

Christmas was brilliant though! We had loads of presents from mum on Christmas day, then saw dad on Boxing Day, and got loads more presents!

After Christmas, I noticed mum and dad would wait until we were in his car with the doors shut, then they would talk on the doorstep. Sometimes they would be quite nice to each other and smile; sometimes they looked cross and sad.

For dad's birthday, we started staying with him for whole weekends. Brilliant! We had such a laugh! Robert was so happy; he was able to play in the park with dad for as long as he wanted, without having to worry about the time.

Following our birthdays in the summer (which were cool and lots of fun – mum and dad both stayed together at our parties, and were nice and smiley to each other), they had one of their 'doorstep chats'. Both looked sad. Dad had dropped us off, and, once his car was out of sight, I asked mum why she was upset. She said that dad wanted something called a 'divorce'. Neither I nor Robert knew what this meant. Mum told us through her tears it meant 'daddy did not want to be married to mummy any more, and that a Judge in a court would make them unmarried.'

For the first time, I felt sad. Robert cried, and asked mum if he could phone dad. Mum called him, and put Robert on. He cried, begging dad to come back and live with us. It was no good, I could hear dad crying down the phone, but he wouldn't come back. Parents are so weird!

Everything carried on OK for a while. We carried on staying with dad at weekends. We got quite used to it to be honest. I did feel sad and guilty sometimes, but we knew dad loved us very, very much, and that's most important of all.

One year after the split, along came the next big event. It was a Friday evening. As usual, we were waiting for dads' car to come into view to take us on our weekend of fun. Whilst we waited, mum said 'daddy has got something to tell you this weekend. I don't want you to ever forget that I am your mum and that I love you both more than anything else in the whole wide world.' She was crying again.

When dad arrived, he was quieter than normal. On the journey to nanny's, I whispered to Robert 'I Bet dad's got a girlfriend, and he's going to tell us!'

I was right!

His girlfriend was a lady called Alice. She had a little boy called Joshua. It felt strange when he told us. We met her the next day. Dad said that if we didn't want to we didn't have to. But we did, because we're nosy.

It was walking up her garden path I suddenly felt nervous, and Robert clung onto to dad's leg. He said we could turn around, but we wanted to see her, despite our nerves.

She was really nice! Joshua was OK too, although a bit younger than us. We stayed for an hour, without leaving dad's side. We went back to nanny's for the rest of the weekend, without mentioning Alice.

Mum wanted to talk about it when we got home, but it upset her when I told her Alice was nice.

I hate one thing about the split, and that's the situation. I hate the thought of hurting mum or dad's feelings. I don't want them to think I'm stupid. Sometimes I feel like it's my fault, and I hate that too. Mum and dad are really good though. I don't know how, but they know when I feel low, so they always do things to make me smile. Dad always tells us he loves us, which really helps too.

We didn't see Alice again for a long time. When we next did, she and dad were living together in their own house. It took a bit of getting used to, and dad never made us feel like we *had* to go there and see Alice all the time. We actually like his house, and really look forward to spending time there.

Mum is OK now I think. She doesn't cry any more, and laughs and smiles a lot. We have moved to a smaller house. It's closer to school, and much warmer in winter. We have a dog too, (dad never let us have one). Robert and I have loads of friends. A lot of their mums and dads have also split up. (Grown ups are worse than kids!)

Mum and dad are divorced, which is sad, although they seem to be friends most of the time. They both come to school plays, sports days and parents' evenings together, and are always together on our birthdays.

Dad recently got *another* new house, which is much bigger, so we have our own rooms at last. We see a lot of nanny and dad's family. We have great fun with dad and Alice, sometimes we see Joshua too and as we are growing up, we are doing more exciting and adventurous things, like going abroad on holidays. Robert still gets sad when dad returns us to mum, but he is OK again pretty quickly.

Finally, when we go to stay with dad, we get to see our baby half-sister, Joy. She is nearly one, and we love her very much – but that's another story altogether …

The Immortal Group plc.

<u>**Manager's Self-assessment**</u>
<u>**learning questionnaire**</u>

For each of the twenty-three competences, assess how well you feel you perform in each of these areas, also the importance of each competence to your current job role. Your response will not be confidential, and will form the basis of any extremely prejudicial action that may be taken against you as a result of this survey.

Please ensure that your name, department and payroll number are clearly printed at the end of this questionnaire, to enable ease of reference for the administration of punitive punishment should the need arise. For simplification of terminology and linguistic interpretation, please ensure your staff are referred to as "they" or "them" at all times. You must ensure you answer clearly and honestly, naming names and deeds should your response appropriate it.

1. <u>Business Awareness</u>

Understands the business, its customers and markets, the way it works, its structure and culture; i.e "every man for himself."

Your Competence:

Fairly competent – can still accept small amounts of responsibility if I am caught unawares.

Job Importance:

Varies between "so important I will die if I get it wrong", to "I really couldn't give a monkey's today."

2. <u>Direct Communication Skills</u>

Conveys ideas and information clearly and in a manner appropriate to the audience, with a high degree of expertise at blaming everyone but yourself when things go wrong.

Your Competence:

So competent, several innocent employees have been ruthlessly discarded and destroyed as a result of my lies when the proverbial has been hitting the fan.

Job Importance:

Number one priority – you never know who may have the knives out for you.

3. <u>Non-Decision making</u>

Evaluates the implications of various options before deciding on a course of action, showing no commitment to and a complete lack of accountability for that decision.

Your Competence:

Very competent – with a proven track record of non-delivery from my decisions, always because someone else has messed it up (Usually HR).

Job Importance:

High – it's the only way to survive in this dog eat dog organization.

4. <u>Developing others</u>

Frightens staff to their full potential, providing timely criticism on performance, setting challenging work assignments and objectives, monitoring progress, whilst ensuring they are doing as they are told without any backchat.

Your Competence:

Excel in it- but only in areas where I will get a direct benefit.

Job Importance:

Focus on what works for me. Look after number 1, it's the first rule of this particular jungle.

5. Financial awareness

Understand the concepts of profit and loss, cash flow and managing budgets in order to use financial information effectively, purely for the health and wellbeing of your own wallet.

Your Competence:

Where my personal interests are concerned – High competence level.

Job Importance:

It's not my money stuck in the Company P+L, and I only influence it when things

go well. When they go wrong, it's because
<u>they</u> have made a mess of it by not doing
as they are told.

6. <u>Human resource management</u>

Understands the impact of, and trends
in, human resource management, and
how they contribute to an organization's
performance management system; ie the
quickest way to terminate with maximum
extreme prejudice.

Your Competence:

Have I been prosecuted yet? No.

Job Importance:

*HR is a fading figment of my imagination;
never referred to, only in times of
historical reminisce. (Except when they
are to be blamed for cocking things up.)*

7. <u>Influencing</u>

Adapts behaviour and communication
style in isolation to gain agreement and
commitment to your ideas and action,
through fair means or foul.

Your Competence:

I am the king of all I survey; no superlative comes close to rating my confidence or capabilities in this area.

Job Importance:

Very High. I tell, <u>they</u> do, and <u>they</u> don't argue.

8. <u>Innovation and creativity</u>

Demonstrates an inquiring mind and encourages new ideas from no one else.

Your Competence:

See Above

Job Importance:

See above. <u>They</u> are not paid to think stuff up. <u>They</u> are paid to do as they are told by me.

9. <u>Dictatorship</u>

Is always able to take charge and adapt own leadership style to suit any situation, to influence and motivate others to perform effectively, usually through fear and intimidation.

Your Competence:

See above and above again. Jesus, do I have to keep repeating myself?

Job Importance:

I lead, <u>they</u> follow. If <u>they</u> don't, <u>they</u> are dealt with. Simple.

10. <u>Managing change</u>

Understands the implications of change in the organizational context, including change for the sake if it, and "mending something that isn't broken" change.

Your Competence:

Excellent. I obediently follow this cultural trait within the organization.

Job Importance:

High – remember, it's about survival and nothing else.

11. <u>Managing cultural differences</u>

Appreciates that cultural differences exist and works to flatten them in order to create effective outcomes, either through diplomatic or "bully boy" channels.

Your Competence:

Recognize small need to change. It's my way or the highway has not filtered to the entire workforce just yet.

Job Importance:

Critical for the future growth of my performance related bonus.

12. <u>Managing information</u>

Appreciates yet ignores the importance and relevance of effective information management, including secrecy, malicious gossip and unauthorised sharing of sensitive data.

Your Competence:

Limited strength. I am unable to keep my mouth shut about anything.

Job Importance:

Not very important – no one else has caught me yet, and if they have, they don't seem to be bothered.

13. <u>Managing Others</u>

Leads the work of others through autocratic dictat to achieve their objectives in the most effective way. Keeps friends close and enemies closer still.

Your Competence:

Excellent – just look at my results.

Job Importance:

Do I really need to say how <u>they</u> should be treated again?

14. <u>Managing the inevitable certainty of uncertainty</u>

Is prepared to move away from familiar ways of thinking and working and deals with uncertain situations comfortably by enhancing uncertainty and fear to create optimum oppressive control.

Your Competence:

Extremely competent.

Job Importance:

Just about as high as it gets.

15. <u>Performance management</u>

Ability to see how ineffective performance management contributes to the delivery of the individual's own strategy in order to survive.

Your Competence:

I'm still here aren't I?

Job importance:

Until I can afford to go – extremely important.

16. <u>Personal effectiveness</u>

Demonstrates excellent procrastination skills by monitoring own performance against politically critical targets and goals.

Your Competence:

World Class – at all times. In fact, I consider myself to be a role model.

Job Importance:

Depends on the size of the decision. The bigger the impact, the more effective the indecisiveness.

17. <u>Political sensitivity</u>

Understands agendas and perspectives of self, recognizes and balances needs of self. Actively adopts "blame" culture at every opportunity.

Your Competence:

Again, I consider myself a role model.

Job Importance:

Not a priority for my personal development – it just comes naturally.

18. <u>Problem enhancing</u>

Creates diversion and denies issues, fails to gather all relevant information, distorts the facts and ignores all possible solutions.

Your Competence:

Again, role model. I am that damn good.

Job Importance:

Essential, especially in the self -preservation game in a large, multi- faceted organization.

19. <u>Process management</u>

Understand the principles of how a morally corrupt business operates, both on a day-to-day and a longer term basis with a view towards people exploitation.

Your Competence:

Clear Strength

Job Importance:

Critical. Maintaining a fragmented sense of security is the only way to keep <u>them</u> alert.

20. <u>Self-development and learning</u>

Takes responsibility and control for everyone else's lack of development and learning; plans for own future direction.

Your Competence:

Improving

Job Importance:

Very Important. We don't want <u>them</u> acquiring knowledge and skills allowing free thought and ideas ... do we?

21. <u>Self-management</u>

Demonstrates self-confidence and assertiveness in all business situations, including inflicting the fear of God in all staff whenever appropriate

Your Competence:

Excellent. Just look at how scared <u>they</u> are when I walk past!

Job Importance:

Critical for growth going forwards.

22. <u>Strategic awareness</u>

Takes an insular view of the business environment, clearly understands business strategy, which should reflect individual, selfish manifesto, forced on an unwilling workforce.

Your Competence:

Judge me by my results

Job Importance:

Only important if it suppresses them.

23. <u>Team destroying</u>

Works well with subordinates, controlling input and participation, only allowing what the Company like to be heard being said.

Your Competence:

Excellent – do you have any complaints?

Job Importance:

Without wishing to boast – this philosophy and my dogged following of this philosophy has kept this company alive for the past ten years. Hasn't it?

Thank you for your time. We will be in touch, sooner than you may think ...

Name: ....

Department: ....

Payroll Number: ....

Transition

'Many of us have times in our life when we act in a way that surprises or even shocks us, Donald. You should consider getting to know your shadow self, it's never too late – even at your age!' Her words were breathlessly delivered; rasped out in short, shallow bursts. They lay side by side, flushed and elated following their recently concluded, all consuming union. Such memories still managed to bring a wry smile to his weary features.

Donald Silverton sat on the rotting wooden bench in the cold, dark chamber, contemplating that memorable hotel room conversation of barely two weeks ago. Rebecca had been one of his leading clients at the time, in so many ways. Her words of wisdom flooded over him as he leant back, supporting himself against the bare, damp concrete wall.

Closing his eyes, he transported himself back to that hotel room of the fortnight past. He remembered lying on the large, ultra comfortable, king-sized bed, upon the jumbled mess of the once tidy crisp linen, now tossed asunder following the frenetic activities of earlier. A cool breeze signalled its arrival via the gentle rustling of gossamer thin curtains, providing little relief to the overriding heat of the day, in turn exacerbated by the overwhelming intensity of their physical exertions. From below, the intrusive cacophony of rush hour traffic invaded his senses through the open window.

'Consider it at least honey!' Rebecca continued, flushed cheeks glistening as she spoke. I can tell you right now, for every person you know who exudes near perfect calm, there is an irrational dark side somewhere just *bursting* to break out. Look at how our so-called celebrities act – spoilt and petulant. The whole lot of them, and they're supposed to be role models to the young for God's sake!'

At that moment, Donald conceded that Rebecca, an ambitious, brash, outspoken, yet brilliantly intelligent professional, didn't have a clue what she was *really* talking about. As a committed bachelor who, through choice, had never settled down with any sort of partner, let alone sire offspring, he could not connect with the visceral emotion she – as an allegedly contented, committed devoted wife and mother of four – displayed at the time.

How different things were now. Vigorously blinking his eyes against the single, piercing shaft of sunlight penetrating the already muted features of the room, he fought to keep in check the stinging tears of frustration building inside, threatening to split him in two. It was his first sign of outward emotion since the incident, and he was glad to be alone, devoid of an audience to share this solitary display of weakness. Once again, his mind returned to the recent, prophetic one-sided exchange of views with Rebecca.

'Whether it's sportsmen or women, pop stars, or fashion models, they all have a dramatic nature, and blow up with the most spectacular tantrums – and that's the ones that do it in public. Imagine how bad things are behind closed doors!' Within her deliberate, silent pauses, the mischievous glint in her simmering eyes spoke volumes. After all, their activities that afternoon represented everything that encapsulated the 'behind closed doors' aspect of her oration. Allowing her playful gaze to linger for a second or two too long for Donald's comfort, she abruptly slid from the rumpled bed, and gently padded across the room to the adjoining cloakroom, firmly locking the door behind her. Despite the unabashed, colourful, intimate and acrobatic style in which she had just shared herself with him, Rebecca still felt compelled to lock the door whilst she answered nature's call. Yet, such was her aura of authority whilst she spoke, even a locked door failed to dilute the gravitas or energy of her proclamations. Donald wondered if his younger client would have such enthusiasm observing the peculiarities of humanity forty years down the line, once the everyday rigours of her chosen career path had also worn her to the very edge of sanity.

'Anyway, we've both got to dash, but remember, it's not just celebs that have a shadow lurking in their psyche my darling. We all do. So don't dismiss it. Not all of us find it so easy to recognize or admit to their 'shadow self' – the hidden 'dark' side we all wish didn't exist. But that doesn't mean we haven't got one. In our chosen profession Donald, it's something we should all be wary of.'

Every single word hollered out from behind that closed door impacted on him, yet only as a conscious thought of denial. He deliberately failed to make the connection as to the intention of her words. As if telepathically sensing this was the case, more words carried through the solid door, pummelling his senses into submission. 'If you are denying you have a hidden side to you ...' The controlled roar of the flush signalled the end of her ablutions, and she re-entered the room to finish the sentence. '… Then what's this all about, I mean, me and you?' She grinned slyly, turned her back to his naked, prone form on the bed, and started creeping around the room, gathering her hastily removed clothes from all four corners of its perimeter.

Once happy every garment had been successfully retrieved, Rebecca quickly redressed without speech, leaving Donald to briefly ponder, then dismiss the theories she had put to him. 'Piffle,' he muttered, dramatically turning over in the bed to ensure he couldn't see her as she carefully adjusted her garments back to their previous immaculate state. Donald had life knowledge and experience – there was simply no substitute for that, or so he reckoned.

'Now, now!' she mocked, her taunt tinged with affection rather than spite. Removing the purse from her leather handbag, she placed five crisp £20 notes onto the dressing table centred against the rear wall. 'Give it some thought at least … you can't stay in denial your whole life you know. If it's really not us, then it may be something you haven't had to face up to yet – but I doubt it.' Moving to where he lay, she bent low, and gently kissed his cheek, murmuring the words he always longed to hear. 'Same time, same date next month?' Despite leaving the room without response, he was confident he actually *heard* her grin as her footsteps brought life to the empty corridor outside, whilst echoing out of his existence for the next four point three weeks.

That afternoon was an eternity ago.

Slumping further into the hard, uncomfortable bench, his sense of isolation was complete. There was no one to call, no one who he could regard as an even remotely close enough friend to share the uncertainty of this current situation. How could he have been so stupid? His professional actions earlier that afternoon had been inexcusable, his inability to adequately explain them rendering him mute. Having lived the bulk of his life in splendid isolation, he was even unable to call upon anyone to vouch for his character. All he had in his favour was an unblemished forty year plus professional record – until a few hours ago.

* * * * *

Donald's date with destiny had been the last Friday in July, and, as with the whole of the month preceding, the country had wilted under the paralysing grip of an unforgiving heatwave.

Having come this far in his career, which had began exactly forty-two years and three months earlier, Donald sat quietly at his desk, counting down the remaining seconds of his career before he left for the final time, to head off into the bold, brave and uninstitutionalised world of retirement – freedom tantalizingly beckoned.

Stinging sweat beads formed at his brow, mildly tormenting him as they frequently trickled into his eyes. Even a failure of the air conditioning system couldn't curb the enthusiasm and excitement building up inside. Leafing through the glossy brochure for the hundredth time that week, his concentration was 95% set on the new car awaiting collection first thing the next morning, and 5% on the heat and usual animated chatter and clattering of desktop keyboards that prevailed at this time of the week. Even though Donald was about to commence a well-deserved, permanent holiday, the others around him were just as excited and distracted by the short-term delights of the impending weekend.

The new Mercedes particularly excited him. For the first time in his life, he indulged in the extravagant luxury of placing an order on a brand new car, assembled to his exacting instructions. No second hand, high miler recycled casts-offs for him this time. Oh no. The healthy slice of financial security gained from his second job – a calling that had come late on in life yet had proven to be very lucrative – more than adequately equipped him to walk into the dealership three months ago, make his demands, then pay outright for the whole thing on the spot. He didn't think he would ever forget the look on the dealer's face – it wasn't very often someone walked in off the street and paid cash up front for a £100,000 executive automobile.

'Have you got any paper?' A male voice interrupted his reverie.

'Pardon?' Donald stared indignantly over his trademark horn rims. The young man before him was impassive.

'My printer's just run out, and I can't find any more.'

Pointing to the open door of the supplies cupboard, Donald's muttered response was merely a disinterested 'help yourself.'

Returning to the brochure, wrapped in thoughts of the fishing holiday due to start as soon as he was ensconced in the new car, Donald noted only twenty minutes remained until freedom arrived.

Settling back, he smiled inwardly as Rebecca cunningly crept into his mind, her presence most welcome, as was always the case on the hundreds of visits she made into his waking thoughts every day. Rebecca. How had he existed for so long without awareness of her presence? If only *she* could be with him, a life partner who brought purpose and meaning to all she connects with.

One year previously, their professions had fatefully brought them together, and the consequences were nothing short of utterly life transforming. Immediate sexual frisson crackled the air, the intensity of their relationship inevitable – the only aspect he failed to understand was the transactional ending every time they co-joined. Yet *her* word of mouth to others spread quickly, and, before truly realizing the nature of his actions, he had a growing client base, entrenched solely within her close, secretive circle of work colleagues. Everything was instigated and managed by this electrical yet hidden companion, proving beyond a doubt that a large market existed for 'unique talent' like him – as long as he 'didn't mention the P word'.

Apparently, it had nothing to do with his physical aspects, but all to do with standard of performance and age. It hadn't taken long for respectable sums of money to accrue, amounts way beyond his retirement plans would provide. Who said no one benefits from ill-gotten gains?

'Sorry, but my hard drive has crashed. Can you take a look at it?'

Glaring disbelievingly at the female hovering over his desk, annoyed at having been wrenched from yet another pleasant daydream for something so petty, Donald wondered if someone was trying to play some sort of final, goodbye joke on him.

'If you're telling the truth, turn the bloody thing off at the server. Someone can sort it out on Monday.' There was absolutely no way on this earth he was going to get involved in a major data recovery exercise at this point. Anyway, he'd been arguing for months that the bulk of equipment was in urgent need of replacement. This more than proved his point.

'But I've got a major project on there. I can't afford to have it lost. I've no back up!' wailed the blonde, who Silverton vaguely remembered her name as Natalie. She was new, and interest in his professional surroundings and all the people within it had all but gone by the time she started at the beginning of the summer season.

'Tough! Now bugger off and leave me alone.'

Natalie stared in jaw-dropping disbelief – yet knew she was going nowhere in her request. Crestfallen, she returned to her workstation, bashing the main server of her PC in total and utter frustration.

With five minutes to go, Silverton felt hot, agitated and impatient. The afternoon had dragged for an eternity, and, for good measure, the others had started to really wind him up. All he wanted was a bit of peace.

'Mr Silverton, please, you'd better come quickly!' It was Natalie again, screaming in horror, staring disbelievingly at her VDU.

Despite always insisting on formalities (he still addressed everyone as either Mr/Mrs/ Miss or Ms), even in these modern times, his tolerance levels had reached the frayed edge of their limits.

'WHAT??' he bellowed. 'WHAT IS IT THAT CAN'T WAIT UNTIL MONDAY?'

He violently stood up, ramrod straight, the force of his action throwing his chair back against the adjacent wall. Feeling his cheeks flush with anger by the second, he marched to the offending workstation.

Peering over Natalie's shoulder, witnesses would later testify to seeing his face immediately shroud in thunderous fury.

On the VDU, a lurid sexual scene between two men, a digital imprint of his face superimposed onto one of the willing participants.

Laughter exploded in the classroom. Class 4M and computer science during final period on Friday afternoons were always a little frisky, yet this obscenity simply broke what was left of Donald's restraint.

An accurate, short sharp punch from the longest serving teacher the school had known – driven with the obliterating force of a piston – immediately crumpled her jaw, silencing the hideous cackling of the fourteen year old girl who taunted him. The laughter stopped, a brief shocked silence punctuated the scene, then the screaming commenced.

Donald sank to his knees, immediately realising the horrendous implications of his craven action, despite the extreme provocation. In the distance of his conscious mind, the school bell rang.

* * * * *

Back in the cell, he kept his eyes firmly closed. Donald was once more thinking of his

234

client cum business manager and yearned for life partner, Rebecca, knowingly teasing him in the hotel room, replaying over and over again the sentence that had, at the time, meant even less to him than anything else that she had said that afternoon.

'Everyone has an aggressive side Donald; it just lies more dormant in some than it does in others. Your usual polite self could disappear at any minute, and a stranger emerges whose aggression could haunt you for the rest of your days. Don't let it take you by surprise, especially in your line of work. You look and sound like you're close to the edge – just hold it together for a few more days ...'

He just knew it would happen, even now, the inevitability and irony was not lost on him. Being honest with himself, he had a strong inkling it would end up exactly like it did – the probabilities were too high from the start. After all, fate – masquerading in the form of retribution – catches up with us all in the end. For the previous twelve months, all the worry and anguish, the heart-stopping fear at the thought of being exposed or caught in the act, had finally come to this.

Being a highly intelligent man – at least in the academic sense – he was acutely aware of Rebecca's own situation, even though she rarely spoke about it. He knew exactly where she was positioned professionally, as well as understanding (but not accepting) the contented wife and mother façade.

In him, she found the father figure who had been absent her entire life, her missing piece. In her, he found respect and a reason to be. She had ignited a torch that he never knew existed in anyone, let alone himself.

A sudden jump in his heart rate greeted the noisy opening of the creaking, foreboding iron door to the containment cell. He had been there for nine hours, yet only now found himself entertaining company for the first time since his incarceration. The arresting officer purposefully strode in, speaking to the wall directly above his head as she addressed him. Neither her words, gestures nor facial expression betrayed emotion. To Donald, it was as if he were being addressed by a corpse.

'Your public defender has arrived. I think you'll agree that you and he need a very long chat …'

Rebecca's dead eyes remained cold and unblinking as she ushered in the court appointed solicitor, her demeanour every bit as inhuman as the room they were gathered in.

Yet beneath that certain death within, Donald felt sure he caught a glimpse of something else in the eyes of the woman he had come to idolise, something so clear and raw, he shouldn't have felt the shock he actually did. As she left the bleak confines of the cell, Rebecca emanated nothing other than a betrayal beyond forgiveness.

For Donald, the worst was only just beginning.

Control

For drinkers at the Lord Nelson pub in the village of Climping, it was a particularly abnormal Sunday. They just didn't know it. Regulars chatted animatedly amongst themselves, enjoying the early spring weather, blissfully unaware of the unfolding catastrophe engulfing their way of life – threatening their very existence.

Half a mile away, within the conference room of the picturesque Granthorpe Hotel, a highly classified, emergency meeting was deep into its fourth hour, the worst fears of those gathered around the large table having been realized.

At the head of the table, David Lang, the harassed chairman, called for order amongst the six attendees for the umpteenth time. Pale beyond the physical possibilities of the human body, denied sleep for forty hours, his demeanour was of a dishevelled, confused, husk of a man. For such a decisive perfectionist, he straddled unknown territory in facing the current unforeseen disaster. His leadership skills and coping strategies were being tested to their absolute limits.

'Jeremy, for the benefit of your learned colleagues in the room, can you please rearticulate your report for all to hear *properly*.' Speaking through tightly clenched teeth, the normally immaculately presented Lang removed his already heavily loosened tie, flinging it to the floor in frustration. Droplets of sweat formed on his shiny, bald skull, yet that didn't stop him running his hands through what remained of silvery wisps of thinning side thatch.

'Very well sir.' The young man to Lang's left, Jeremy Wolfton, adjusted his steel rimmed glasses, nervously fiddled with his tie knot, then cleared his throat to address the now still attendees, ready to hang on to his every word.

'As I said earlier ...' his presence lacked projection or impact, his voice thin and reedy. The contents of his update more than compensated in keeping everybody's attention. '... The tests have proved conclusively the influenza virus had been found in a live specimen for the first time. More than 150,000 specimens in the surrounding area are about to be slaughtered as a precautionary measure ...'

Uproar shattered the tranquillity once again.

'Good God man!' Major Patrick Savage, the armed forces representative, banged his fist on the table with alarming force. 'Why does it have to be so many? Can we be sure about this? If the media or public ever found out about this there ...'

'SIT DOWN AND LET HIM FINISH!' Lang bellowed at the army man. 'That goes for the rest of you ...' he sighed deeply, and stepped from his chair, turning his back to gaze beyond the panelled patio doors, onto the beauty of the untousled British countryside in springtime. '... just listen. Continue Jeremy.'

'Yes sir ... As I said, we are about to commence extermination as a precautionary measure. As we speak, the army are assisting the facility workers in removing all condemned specimens to the incarceration plant sixty miles west in the market town of Naresborough.'

'How many facility workers are delivering this piece of work?' David Niles, the country's leading Environmental Health Officer asked, his tone functional, detached from the emotion of the reality.

'100 all vaccinated at the emergency clinic set up on the border of the protection zone. Obviously, they are concerned about their own health, but all measures are being taken to safeguard and protect their wellbeing.' With a further fidget of his tie, Wolfton sat, his legs barely able to hold him up any longer.

'Mr Chairman, if I may be so bold to ask?' Rachel Gardner, council leader for the affected area politely raised her hand, yet her glaring eyes suggested a ticking bomb was ready to detonate beneath her calm exterior.

'Certainly Mrs Gardner, please continue.' Lang resumed his seat at the head of the table.

'I am curious as to how we will be able to keep the media at bay. The protection zone is so … vast, and the numbers we are talking about are catastrophic. I would urge we seriously consider going public before events overcome us.'

'Thank you Mrs Gardner. Your concerns are duly noted for the minutes.'

'There's no one taking notes you charlatan!' The Major again shot up from his seat, remonstrating furiously at Lang.

Ignoring him, he turned to the calmest person in the room, his personal assistant and most trusted confidant, Cliff Bowyer. Bowyer hunched over an endlessly clicking laptop, processing frantic numbers of emails transmitting from the protection zone, with updates by the minute. 'Are we any clearer with the sequence of events since all this started?'

'Well sir, based on all the data available so far …'

'Just spit it out man!' The Major's patience frayed to breaking point.

'As I *was* saying.' Bowyer's irritation was obvious. 'The outbreak began last Tuesday with the sudden death of seventeen examples. Initially, staff in the vicinity did not suspect the virus. Young specimens are particularly susceptible to a varying number of diseases at this time of year, and the deaths were not seen as cause for alarm.'

The room fell into silence. Only the military man demonstrated outwards signs of disgrace towards the whole appalling situation. The P.A. continued.

'Over the next two days, a further one thousand perished. At 6 pm on Thursday, the Chief Environmental officer here …' he raised his eyebrows in the direction of Niles, '… and his team of experts were called in.'

'Is this true Mr Niles? Two days after the original deaths?' The chairman looked directly at the Environmental Officer, eyes tempered with controlled aggression. Niles' response was succinct and professional.

'Yes sir. It is. However, despite the obvious concerns a two day time lag in a case such as this may cause, I assure you that any virologist or specialist in the field will tell you this is not an unusual or unreasonable response time when taking into account the low mortality rates in the area.'

'OK ... I will go along with your explanation ... for now.' The Major and the Council Leader both slumped in their chairs, unable to escape from the horrific events that brought them here in the first place.

'Mr Bowyer, please continue.'

'Thank you sir. By Friday morning, with the Environmental team in attendance, the deaths had climbed to 2,600, with an estimated 4,500 now showing signs of illness upon random inspection. Carcasses were removed to a secure holding area, where blood tests and swabs were taken for analysis at our research facility in Sussex. It was at this point, the discussion as to whether we should cull or not first surfaced.'

The room remained still.

'At 6 pm on Friday, a two mile cordon was placed around the epicentre of the outbreak, where all specimens were kept indoors and tested. At 9 pm, the original cordon was surrounded by a six mile 'surveillance' zone, whereby all specimen movement was curbed. At 6 am yesterday morning, Saturday, we received the results from the Sussex facility confirming our worst fears. An immediate 807 square mile 'protection zone' was set up with full 24 hour round the clock monitoring.' Bowyer stopped for breath, feeling his hand shake slightly as he concluded. 'At 3 am this morning, following a full back-up screening and security analysis of the samples from Sussex, Mr David Niles advised you of the need to slaughter all 154,000 specimens as a matter of urgency to avoid the contamination spreading further.'

'Thank you, Mr Bowyer,' Lang whispered.

'Mr Niles, what is the prognosis once the slaughter is complete?'

'Very good, Prime Minister. I am 100% that once this remedial action is completed, there will be no further danger, and the outbreak will be successfully contained.'

'Thank you. Mr Wolfdon?'

'Yes, Prime Minister?' he mumbled, fearful of the next command.

'As Secretary of State of State for Defence, I would like to ensure that you work closely with Major Savage. Ensure we deal with the actual destruction of so many of Her Majesty's innocent subjects with compassion and humility.'

He stood, slowly and deliberately. 'Mrs Gardner, Mr Niles, you will be coming with me.'

'Prime Minister?' the Environmental officer looked on quizzically.

'You are both coming with me to address the media. We are going public right now. Mrs Gardner, you will stand with me whilst Mr Niles here explains to the world the absolute necessity for the action we have taken. Never before should mankind have to face up to the horrors of what we have sanctioned this weekend ...'

'Prime Minister Lang, I must object ...'

'Mr Niles, you will not object. I suggest you tidy yourself up. Mrs, Gardner, please come with me to the video conferencing room, I would like you to speak directly with Her Majesty, who will be waiting to offer her condolences for the souls of those departed, and the loss of your once great city.'

The Fabulous Life?

It wasn't the eerie tranquillity of the serene, immaculate beach playing on his mind. It wasn't the moral discomfort he felt just by lying here, on his privately owned, twenty-two mile stretch of white sand, framed by a azure blue sea gently kissing the cheeks of the shoreline. It wasn't even the enormous, built to personal specification thirty-six bedroom villa behind him, casting its monumental shadow across the westerly end of *his* beach. Even the fact that, grotesque as it was, this entire island in the remotest of outposts in the Caribbean, belonged entirely to him, Stephen Nausbaum was not yet having the crisis of conscience over his unimaginable and gargantuan personal wealth. That would come later. It always did.

No, right now, sitting upright on an air-cushioned sun lounger, taking in the sight of his well-stocked marina to the left, resplendent with four 100ft plus yachts – of the highest specification – and the two helicopter pads at either end of the sprawling floating harbour, right now it was a much more fundamental question that slowly burned away inside, threatening to incinerate his very soul.

What was it all about? What was the point of it all? His internal debates challenging the purpose of life and existence maintained the source of an endlessly deep and intense continuation for the wealthiest human being who ever walked the face of planet earth.

Only last month, one of his many well-remunerated accountants had delightedly informed him via videophone that his dozens of personal bank accounts now bulged with over $43 trillion, with the balance sheet increasing by $5 billion annually. 'Should things continue as they are, and there's no reason not to …' this particularly shrewd bean counter had delightedly gloated through the real time plasma screen, '… you will be the wealthiest global entity within a decade.'

'What do you mean by *entity*?' He whispered in shocked response, aghast by the calculating tone of his advisor. 'It's simple, Stephen. By that time, your personal assets will outweigh the GDP of every single nation on earth. You …' He never caught the rest, his head unable to comprehend the madness of it all.

Now, lying back once more, closing his eyes in contemplation at the memory of that uncomfortable exchange, Stephen immersed himself in the surrounding delights of its environment. Gentle waves lapped the shore as the ocean deliciously tossed and turned, complemented by a warm, throaty rumble. Grabbing a handful of warm sand, he basked in the exquisite sensation of the fine, textured particles gently bouncing through the webbing of his fingers.

A gentle breeze caressed his furrowed brow, rattling and rustling the overhead leaves of the giant palm trees that acted as a natural shield, protecting him from the curiosities of an inquisitive outside world.

Despite the glamour and exuberance of the location, the sea air here was no different than any other part of the planet where land met a vast expanse of unbridled water, therefore, there was a familiar, yet delicious saltiness crackling in the atmosphere, tantalizingly brushing his senses of smell and taste.

Was this part of the answer? Experiencing unhampered nature as our creator intended? After all, human life was such a fragile, organic existence – nothing but an organism in the greater, mind-blowing scheme of what we understand to be the universe – insignificant yet self-sufficient. What, ultimately, was the purpose or justification for our being? You are born, the end result of the miraculous act of human creation. You live a life, an existence for a random, indiscriminate period of time. You die. That's it. Whilst our physical hearts pump life through our veins, and the enormous cluster of cells known as the brain instruct the heart what to do, Stephen still struggled with the entire aspect regarding purposeful existence. After all, all he needed to do was look at himself for the ultimate addition to his harrowing inner turmoil.

Regardless of his unimaginable wealth, he was the most commonly talked of un-famous famous person in the world. Globally, he was an invisible icon; the reference point for all that is good in mankind to aspire to. Everyone, absolutely *everyone*, knew his name, as they also recognized his celebrated, phenomenal wealth. Not one penny of it was ever begrudged. The only person within the current population of the human race who openly challenged the vulgarity relating to the vastness of his bank account was Stephen himself. Last year alone, trying to atone for his self-amassed yet burdensomely guilt-inducing fortune, he donated $15 billion cash to various global good causes. The result merely cemented his immortality from a global public who already revered him as a God, not a man. In every corner of every continent, he was referred to as the 'giver of life'. Religious organizations had formed, reaching a rapid pre-eminence against the backdrop of his staggering legacy for civilisation. His mere existence challenged the very fundamentals of Christianity – for a believing majority, he was the new messiah.

Yet no one really knew who he actually was. Never, ever seen in public to be adequately photographed or recorded, his anonymity only served to fuel the enigma surrounding him. Often, he wondered of the catastrophic fallout should the day come where he would finally be exposed as a normal human being who bled, farted, yawned, belched, pissed and shit just like everyone else. After all, the revelation that your God had such human qualities would be destabilising for millions. Wouldn't it?

So, what *was* the point in the human urge to generate and retain wealth for such material comforts? He was continually tortured by the intense complexities of his own questions. Why did people work so hard all their lives only to spend their hard earned on luxurious labour saving devices? After all, when time was called, none of the accumulations from life's labours could be taken beyond – wherever or whatever *that* particular existence is. All accomplishments whilst serving time on this mortal coil were well and truly null and void once we shuffle from it. So, amongst the very essence of why we exist, why make such an effort in the first place?

Stephen frowned at the thought of the millions, billions even, of unseen, unknown worshippers at the altar of his greatness. Every single one of them unbeknown of the inner turmoil and vexatious state of thinking that occupied the mind of their idol.

And what of the countless many, toiling daily with the overriding objective of achieving a standard of life which was infinitesimal in its minuteness compared to the grandeur enjoyed by the rich and super rich of the planet? Theirs was an existence glamorised by many, viewed upon as impossibly unreachable trinkets in a jeweller's shop window, by keen, eager, yearning, pleading misshapen faces, squashed by the pressure of the glass against their skin.

Keeping his visual senses at bay, relying on his heightened kinaesthetic and auditory filters, Stephen instead visualised some of his own personal 'trinkets', all advised upon as 'good business' by his ever-increasing, expensively assembled army of accountants and solicitors, yet only amassed since the sudden accumulation of his numerical fortune.

Here on the island, not only could he call the vast house his own personal property. The grand marina and purpose built, private airport complete with self-contained terminal, restaurant, shops and a hotel (not forgetting six fully crewed jetliners on standby twenty-four hours a day), were all his, bought and paid for in hard cash.

The house here on the island itself was a modest piece in his global portfolio of private dwelling places. At 25,000 sq ft, with twenty bedrooms , seven kitchens, sixteen bathrooms, a full size cinema auditorium, mini nightclub, private sixteen table restaurant, four informal bars, a wine and cheese tasting room (all the rage – apparently), ten lane bowling alley, sixty immaculately manicured acres of gardens and futuristic property security bristling with patents and innovations unlikely to be used by NASA for at least a decade (until its technology caught up), – it represented nothing more to Stephen than a hateful reminder of consumerism and materialism completely bereft of its senses. With an interior décor including the finest hand-made deep pile Persian carpets with Italian marble and hand-rolled gold leaf throughout, the whole place made him feel physically sick. Yet he had personally ordered and paid for its construction – because he could.

Morally, the only positive aspect of the house he was happy to justify were the 300 permanent staff it employed, twenty-four hours a day, 365 days of the year, all on wages vastly more superior than anything else they would find within their own employment marketplace. Throw in the additional 400 ancillary support staff including the marina and airport personnel, and they represented the wealthiest socio-economic group within their national population. They only saw their master for three weeks a year – although Stephen's very ordinary guests were also feted as royalty whenever he 'loaned the place out.' Therefore, despite his personal revulsion, he would never sell – a whole economy was built around him. He was needed.

Sighing deeply, he drowned in his thoughts, completely immersed within the prison of his vast mind.

Thirteen other private houses, 10–100,000 sq ft each, spanned the globe. He once paid $36 million above the asking price for one particular property because he liked the way it appeared in a photograph. Not forgetting that he was still to visit it, or three of his other homes for that matter.

Five years ago, for no other reason than to provide employment in a depressed area, he had a small, mock far eastern country built on 100 acres of disused wasteland, constructed to his exact, demanding specifications. 500 men a day, over four years, at a cost of $700 million had delivered it, all from lavishly expensive architects' drawings, solicitors and god knows who else's plans. The end 'benefits' to this opulent project included a forty-three bedroom 70,000 sq ft mansion, 1,000 generously remunerated permanent staff (another moral winner he supposed), an artificial lake – complete with a full compliment of exotic sea life, pier, bridge, and jet ski berth – 64 track recording studio, two cinemas, a restaurant+ nightclub, helipad, twelve hand tiled mosaic swimming pools, an international airport length runway with terminal building (plus the three jets of course), and seventy-three miles of fibre optic cabling underground to support the mind-blowing technology ensuring every nuance of this staggering estate were automated, and the world's most valuable and palatial piece of real estate was a dwelling fit for any serving royal family.

Since receiving the keys to this particular property, Stephen had visited twice, spending the best part of one month physically occupying it. For the remainder, it stood empty, a monument to the grotesque that even the closest of his associates knew nothing of.

As the sun gently glided towards the horizon, irresistibly drawn by the pull of late evening, Stephen remained still, deep in contemplation. A fiercely private and humble man, his obscene wealth weighed him down like an albatross around his neck. His life, his precious, limited piece of being, was not predestined for this. Something had gone wrong in the programme. His time was earmarked as one of vocation and sacrifice, anonymous toiling for the greater benefit of his fellow men.

To that end, once he realized his calling as a highly advanced, academically gifted eight year old over forty years ago, his chosen path became clearly defined, and he embraced his lifestyle of servitude with aplomb.

Throughout his formative student years, into adulthood, isolation, coupled with obsessive application to his work meant no time for friends, family, relationships or children. As an only child himself, the genetic bloodline ended with him, his legacy bound in science, befitting for all mankind.

Slowly standing, stretching creaky limbs, opening his eyes, marvelling at the pure purple sunset as the remaining splinters of orange sunlight triumphantly broke through whilst the night continued to claim this half of earth as its own, Stephen's unsettled conscience once again reminded him that the most rewarding elements of our insignificant existence are entirely free.

It was time for him to change direction. For so long, his real desire had been thwarted by the endless armies of hangers-on. But he was stronger now – experienced enough to understand the true meaning of the richness of life – and vast sums of money had nothing to do with it. Action was needed, and now was as good a time as any. First thing tomorrow, against the advice and wishes of those jackals who advised him so diligently in the accumulation of his hollow fortunes, his entire estate – every single one of those trinkets and baubles – would be served notice of ownership. He would not negotiate. The team of reptilian property lawyers would not dare go against his wishes, no matter how volumatic their protestations, he was their meal ticket and he knew it.

The paralysing anguish had gone on long enough. Guilt was a heavy, obsessive cross to bear. His conscience had crippled for long enough. There would be no turning back from his decision.

Finding a spring in his step for the first time in a decade, Dr Stephen Nussbaum, multiple Nobel Prize winner, smiled. For the man who had sacrificed his entire life in sole pursuit of seeking the cures for the great medical scourges that had so long had been a blight on the face of humanity, yet alone medical science, he was happy once more, immediately relieved of his great burden. He wished he had followed through the courage of his convictions before. The lawyers would be outraged. They would howl and scream – but that was their problem, not his.

Creating the artificial remedies to cure all known cancers had delivered the pinnacle of all he lived and breathed for. Thwarting one of nature's 'great evils' vindicated everything. Unknown to him, his material validation came in the form of immediate wealth as a result of a single, lucrative patent, initially designed to 'protect the work', yet he now understood the motives of those who had advised him. Immediately, his existence became cloaked in deeper isolation, misery and self-doubt. Life became a non-stop traversal across the fringes of humanity, guiltily entrenched in the furthest reaches of civilisations sidelines.

Despite his removal from normality, his global adoration and worship as a God, was unchallenged, unmatched and without parallel in status. Such fanatical emotions in others merely brought him nothing more than a stunted mind and crises of conscience – an overbearing distraction.

But no more! Rebuking himself for allowing matters to take so long in coming to action, he entered his soon to be ex-holiday home through a small entrance to the rear, as was normal.

There was a lot to be said for such a gluttonous property portfolio, especially when first thing the next morning, every single one of them, and all that came within, would be announced to the world, by him, as pre-treatment centres, specialised hospices or post-treatment convalescence homes. In addition, he would announce that the remainder of his wealth should be set up in controlled trusts, to oversee the construction of identical centres worldwide, fully equipped and staffed whilst funded and maintained from his own pocket.

No stone was to be left unturned in delivering this vision. The capability and infrastructure already existed to make it happen – the current houses were testimony to that.

Stephen was about to reclaim his life as his own, his purpose re-ignited, back on the vocation road once more.

Sitting at the desk of an expansive study, he started to write. The action lists – and there would be many – would act as a suitable therapy in the healing process. Dawn beckoned, merely a few hours away, signalling the start of a new day – and with it another new beginning for humankind.

Star

Jonathan was only stood upright for a few seconds before he buckled and crumbled against the wall. Unable to control the rising nausea and violent trembling in his arms and legs, he was grateful that at least his fall had been broken – even if a little uncomfortably. Protectively crossing his arms over his chest, the sweat from his palms began soaking their way through the flimsy white fabric of his long sleeved shirt. Somewhere in the distance of his own awareness, he could even hear his teeth chattering.

'Why don't you sit down sir?' one of the uniformed policemen asked from the other side of the grey, threadbare office. He was leaning against the large desk occupying most of the floor space of the tiny room, admiring several photographs of two young children dotted across its surface. Jonathan ignored the request. Having them here in the room only made things worse, yet it was an inevitable part of the process. Now it was the turn of the second one, a little shorter and chubbier than his athletically built colleague. 'Really sir, the manager will be here in a couple of minutes, and we can sort everything out.'

In normal circumstances – whatever normal actually stood for these days, Jonathan would have ignored him too. However, this one carried a small handgun, tucked neatly into a very visible holster slung under his left arm. Probably best not to argue with an armed lawman. He nodded, and without a word or eye contact, nervously shuffled onto the remaining upright chair in the room.

Outside, thunder rumbled earthwards from an unsettled, swirling black sky. Such was its volume; even the policemen were forced to take a slight glance heavenwards out of the tiny window that provided the only glimpse of natural light within the confines of the cramped room.

Closing his eyes, desperately trying to rein in the uncontrollable shakes threatening to splinter his very soul, Jonathan commenced his routine of deep breathing exercises reserved for the increasing number of occasions similar to this one. As he methodically took in great, voluminous, gasping lungfuls of air, the two policemen looked at each other, unsympathetically rolling their eyes heavenwards. As far as they were concerned, the store manager could not arrive quickly enough. It was always the same with these types.

Still fighting the raging demons within, Jonathan cursed inwardly for allowing himself to become so compromised, to reach such a low point. After all, every life choice he had made up to now was responsible for getting him here. Nothing about this current union – with two unknown policemen in a pathetically maintained office belonging to the manager of a well-known store in a completely strange and alien town – had come about by accident. It was all by design, ambition and purpose. Inwardly, he cursed himself for pursuing such a warped and twisted ambition.

The door burst open as a young twenty something ball of energy, all spiky gelled hair and designer suits, danced into the room, profusely apologising for being late. 'Sorry to keep you gents waiting – it's absolutely manic down there!' The 'down there' was the mid-December frenzy of the sales floor, a million miles removed from the stillness of the room the four men occupied, despite residing in the same building. Two worlds were instantaneously colliding under one roof.

'Great,' Jonathan muttered. More people invariably meant greater humiliation. Yet he knew he only had himself to blame. The store manager shifted uncomfortably, uncertain of where to take the conversation with his 'guest'.

From his formative years, through to young adulthood, Jonathan had been singularly determined in the pursuit of his chosen speciality. Such was its uniqueness, no one ever thought he could scrape a living from it, let alone carve out a brilliant career. In the early days, this was the case, where despite his best and most industrious efforts, constant setback and failure coursed through his chosen occupation. Yet he persevered.

Once the inevitable success arrived, so too the notoriety. To the unsuspecting world at large, the breakthrough had come swiftly and suddenly. To those in the know, Jonathan's overnight recognition had taken a dozen years. Suddenly, his anonymity was gone, his privacy stripped bare. People would stare and point in the street, Police followed him with every step he took. He was unable to walk through any sort of public place without having security guards monitor every move. And that didn't even include the intrusiveness of the cameras that appeared form out of nowhere on every corner he turned.

Then there was this, the countless, endless occasions where he had ended up in the manager's office of a particular store accompanied by the police, awaiting a decision. How he abhorred this existence.

He was brought out of this reflection of misery by the store manager clearing his throat. 'Despite the craziness of the situation, the reason the store is so packed is because of you.' He looked directly at Jonathan as he spoke. 'So unless you want to pull out now, and disappoint the hundreds down there who have queued for hours to meet you, let's go.'

Reluctantly, he rose to his feet, and, as was usual, the shaking began ebbing away, in small, gratifying waves of relief.

'OK sir?' the taller policeman asked him, feigned concern in his voice. He had seen it all before.

'Fine,' Jonathan whispered. The policeman turned to the manager. 'Right then. You lead the way, and we will escort Mr Blade through the store. I assume there is a strong presence from the local press?'

'Yes …' the young manager confirmed, eyeing his special guest nervously, '… but the nationals are here too.'

'It's to be expected!' The shorter, armed officer chortled. 'Let's go then!'

Furiously clenching and unclenching his fists, desperately encouraging circulation back into his fingers, Jonathan Blade, the world's most often read author of crime fiction, one of the most recognizable men on the planet, was led onto the main sales floor of the largest bookshop in the world, on a rare public appearance to meet his adoring, devoted fans.

It had only been upon the publication of his fifth and most recent title, *Star*, that he had been elevated into the literary stratosphere, being placed in the gods of 'worldwide blockbuster author' fame. The only unspectacular aspect of his story was the story itself – a reworking of the formulaic 'boy with nothing makes it big then loses it all again' – coupled with a plagiarised plot in criminal activity.

Unfortunately for him, it was also the exact same time that the chronic shyness and subsequent physical aversion to being in the presence of strangers invaded his life, occupying him as an unshakeable disease, crucifying any connectivity from the very people with whom he had been so desperate in reaching out to.

Sitting gingerly between the massed piles of his books before the screaming, waving hordes that had waited for anything up to twelve hours to meet him, with thousands of watts of media flashbulb lights simultaneously exploding in his face, Jonathan Blade wondered if it had all been worth it.

❦

Taunt

'It's on at two five nine, nine fifty.' The young estate agent spoke without emotion, displaying next to no interest in the property he was trying to sell her. It was exactly the sort of behaviour that gave his profession such a dismal perception in the 'people you trust the least' league.

'Can we have a quick look around it then?' Jackie's patience was already wearing thin. Now in their third property of the morning, he had done absolutely nothing to enthuse her – he was more interested in generating chatter through his constantly ringing bright red mobile phone than trying to sell her a house. Unbelievably, it was somewhere between the kitchen and dining room of the hideous second property that he had attempted to break the ice with a token, 'I'm Daniel, by the way …'

As they stood on the doorstep, he had one foot over the threshold of the entrance porch to the small terraced property. Jackie stood outside, gently simmering as he caught a glimpse of his reflection in a grubby window pane, stopping to quickly adjust his black, hideously gelled spiky hair. 'I *said* …' Jackie was now speaking a little too loudly, a little too forcefully as, not for the first time that day, he interrupted her.

'Of course *madam!*' He positively forced the words from his lips as his attitude grew increasingly reptilian by the minute. Following him across the threshold, along the small, brightly decorated hallway, they entered a tiny yet immaculately decorated living room.

'I can tell you that they turned down an offer of two four nine flat about a month ago, so you may want to bear that in mind.' Once again, his hand slithered through the preposterously oily black thatch whilst he disinterestedly eyed the small, cream leather sofa occupying two thirds of the floor space in the room.

'Thanks.' Jackie smiled curtly. 'I will.' Having seen enough of this particular room, quickly scanning the rest of the property, getting out and getting away from this thoroughly unpleasant jackal of a human being was her main priority. 'Can I take a quick look around?' She felt uncomfortable with the request – the owners were absent, yet despite their knowledge of the viewing, a certain sense of intrusion, even violation occupied the back of her mind.

'Sure.' He plonked himself on the inviting sofa, flipping open the infernal phone without so much as looking at her. 'The vendor is at work, the place is empty …' His face was a picture of concentration as he jabbed at the tiny illuminated buttons. '… help yourself and take your time.'

'Why … *Thank you!*' Quietly mooching to the base of the stairs in the increasingly claustrophobic hallway, she could not decide if Daniel was the absolute worst she had ever come across. Of all the vultures masquerading as estate agents she had seen during the past six weeks, he was definitely in the bottom two. It was a close call between him and the guy from yesterday. *His* outlook and professional courtesy had been more pleasant than the young reprobate now lolloping around in the next room, in someone else's property – someone's home. No, yesterday's reptile (she thought his name might have been Kurt) had blatantly and unsettlingly overused her name. 'As you can see Jackie, this is a brand new kitchen,' and 'Jackie, I'm going to leave you to have a quick look around by yourself whilst I make a call, yeah?' or 'So what are your thoughts, Jackie?' and so on and so on.

How she had absolutely detested that over-familiar creep! In her list of personal cardinal sins, a stranger over-using her name was up there on a par with some bastard quite literally breathing down your neck. Luckily, even by the low standards of the cretins she had come into contact with looking for a new home, none of them had plummeted to that particular depth. Yet. After this amount of time with them, she felt confident she knew all the different versions.

Reaching the top landing after a rapid ascent, dutifully poking her head into two double bedrooms (both immaculate), bathroom (newly fitted in a tasteful aqua and diamond white arrangement), and airing cupboard (neat and well organized), Jackie knew that despite being stood in a very well maintained and much loved home, she would not be putting in an offer. Mainly because of Daniel – she would give his office manager a thorough piece of feedback – but also due to a lack of practicality.

Every property she'd viewed to date had been far too small! Prices in the city were staggering. Despite the inconvenience likely to be caused in her professional life, she had already decided to look further afield, beyond the central conurbations, where considerably increased amounts of bricks and mortar could be purchased for a similar shilling.

Quietly closing the bathroom door, respectful of the care and attention placed into the high standards of maintenance, she paused at the top stair, temporarily lost in further considerations.

'DANIEL ...' she called firmly yet politely down the stairs, her voice floating ethereally, resonating through the limited inner space of the property. '... can I just check something with you please?' Her intention was for *him* to come to *her*. Despite her displeasure at the aloofness of this utterly dislikeable young man, she was still his prospective client. And she had a significant advantage – Jackie was seriously moneyed.

Her wallet was literally overflowing, having – to use Daniel's primitive dialect – 'quarter of a mil burnin' a hole in her pocket.' The money was hard-earned and well-deserved, the result of being awarded the biggest single contract of her career. As usual, she had a strong urge, an irresistible compulsion to spend it. Even as a child, much to the chagrin of her parents, if she had £5 pocket money to spend, she would spend as long as she could in a shop, having selected an item for £4 within a minute, then spend the next half an hour looking for that something special that would relieve her of the awkward remaining £1.

All of her life, whenever she had buying power, it excited and thrilled her. Right now, she was the beholder of the highest type of buying power she had ever known, making sure these ne'er-do-well estate agents knew about it in the process.

'Yes madam?' Daniel huffed, having appeared as if by magic at the bottom of the stairs. He had removed his jacket and loosened his tie The bright red phone was clutched protectively in his left hand. He looked like an errant schoolboy disturbed in a prohibited conversation.

'There appears to be something wrong with the particulars,' She provocatively waved the A4 descriptive details before her, as if a fan keeping tropical heat at bay.

'What do you mean?' he barked, as a prickly halo of intense frustration emanated his from every pore.

Enjoying herself in the knowledge that she had now suddenly turned the tables on him, she continued, mockingly reading from the particulars.

'Well, according to this,' she pointed theatrically at the scrunched up piece of paper, '… there is *supposed* to be a fully fitted bedroom/study room. Of a southerly aspect, this versatile area, measuring 5' x 5' provides an ideal, quiet self-contained study area, as well as adequately transforming into a suitable guest room or bedroom four solution for a growing family.' Her eyes never left his as she carefully, deliberately slowly folded the the sheet back into perfect quarters. 'So where is this box room?' she taunted him in pitch and tone now, dramatically placing her hand on her hip as she spoke. 'I can't see it anywhere up here!'

Daniel returned her stare in utter, incredulous disbelief. Unblinking, he brought the red phone handset to his ear, muting his voice as he calmly told the invisible friend at the other end of the line, 'Something's come up. I'll call you later.' Flipping the handset shut, he took a deep breath to control his rapidly rising urge to physically assault this cocky mare of a woman. Instead, he just bellowed.

'That's impossible! Let me see!' His voice was well and truly at its most animated since she met him, and the urgency in which he ascended the staircase demonstrated his complete discomfort at her allegation. 'It's just not possible!' he stammered, snatching the document from Jackie's outstretched hand. 'I wrote these particulars myself. I ...' he started to carefully review the now unfolded sheet, pouring over every nuance of every sentence, every room dimension.

Suppressing a sly grin, Jackie knew this would be a wonderful comeuppance for the cocky little gobshite. Oh, how she was going to teach him a lesson for disrespecting her!

Usually, her viewings had at least elicited polite comment or conversation from agents and vendors alike (even the hideous guy from the previous day). 'Do you mind if I ask what you do for a living?' was her personal FAQ, usually asked by the women. Such interest in her, and the aura of pure independence she generated, gave her an immense source of personal pride and heightened self-esteem. There was always a crackle in the air when others met a self-made woman, who had got to where she was by getting her hands dirty by pure hard graft. She was the first to realize the difference it made.

Daniel quickly danced through the first floor rooms, agitated and swearing aloud, looking for an explanation or excuse, no matter how sensational. Anything to avoid the admission of a mistake would be acceptable; after all, his one dimensional sense of personal pride was at stake.

'Steady on!' Jackie beamed, purposefully selecting her words. 'Calm down! It's not as if anyone died in here, is it!' She gently brushed his arm as he stumbled by, timing the physical contact to perfection. In turn, by way of reflex, he withdrew from her, avoiding any sense of physical proximity, hastily marching into the nearest adjacent room.

Standing in the middle of bedroom two, he abruptly relayed his triumphant conclusion. 'Obviously, they've knocked the two rooms into one since these particulars were drafted.' He paused, waiting for a response. None came. 'Therefore', he carried on, encouraged by the wall of silence, 'the vendor has failed to inform us of these adjustments. Still, it shouldn't be a big job if you want to put the wall back in!' His cheesy smile dared Jackie to retaliate in an exercise of equally quick thinking.

His bare-faced gall knew no bounds. Who or what on earth did he think he was?

'I wont lie to you.' He emerged from the room in triumph. 'That third bedroom was nothing but a glorified cupboard, but you knew that anyway.'

She screwed up her face in concentration. This nasty little piece of work, this officious little deceiver needed to be taught a lesson. He had no right to carry on regardless in such an appalling manner.

'Are we finished here then?' Impatience returned to his voice as he flipped open the bright red squawkbox.

'Yes, Thanks. The trip has been … worthwhile.' Despite her reservations, and the challenges to her own professional morals and ethics, she had decided *exactly* what she was going to do with him.

'Good. I just need to …' Jackie finished the sentence for him. 'Make a call?'

'Yeah. Make a call.' He looked down his nose at her, as if she were something unpleasant he had trodden in. 'And then we'll leave.' He shuffled towards the bathroom door, unzipping his fly with one hand, clamping the phone to his ear with the other. So, he could speak on the phone whilst answering the call of nature! How unique – a man who could multi-task!

Nodding her understanding, she slowly descended the stairs, placing herself at the entrance hall, where she could be guaranteed to hear every nuance of his reaction to her act of retribution. Smiling inwardly, she was unable to hide her heightened sense of anticipation at what was about to happen. Something he would live with for the remainder of his days. It was seconds away …

It was a terribly ugly sound as his feminine screams filled the air. He literally flew from the bathroom, and staggered down the stairs with flies still undone (thankfully his member was out of view), in a complete state of flux. He blindly grabbed for her, breathing hard, eyes bulging in panic and fear.

Bingo! She'd hit the bull's eye. However, her smug sense of self-righteousness was quickly eradicated by the sudden sharp pain of Daniel clumsily stamping on her sandalled foot. He was preoccupied by his trembling hands as they uncontrollably jabbed at the buttons of his phone console.

'Jesus Christ! Oh My God!' he stammered.

'What on earth is wrong?' she hissed, angrily clutching her foot, as waves of throbbing pain coursed through it.

'Jesus Christ! Jesus! Jesus! Jesus!'

She slapped him on the cheek, catching him flush in one swift move. 'DANIEL!' He immediately came to; shock temporarily leaving him, and his frightened eyes met her steely gaze. Desperately trying to control his enforced stammer, he spat the words out as if learning to speak all over again.

'Upstairs. The bathroom. A man. Dead. In the bath. Blood everywhere … Jesus … Gotta call the police …' He lurched away, shaking uncontrollably as clinical shock took hold of his senses.

'Take me up and show me.' She sounded soothing, almost compassionate, yet grinned slyly as he slumped in the far corner of the hallway with his back to her.

'No way, I'm calling the police. Jesus! The dead guy, it's … it's … it's the vendor!' he spat the words out forcefully yet disbelievingly.

'Oh for Christ's sake! Are you mad?'

He abruptly swung back to face her, flecks of anger now tingeing those panicked eyes. 'Of course I'm fucking sure!' he blurted. 'How could you have missed it?'

'I think your imagination has run wild young man.' She was doing all she could to suppress the building well of laughter from deep within. 'Before you make that call, let me take a look.'

'Be my guest,' he spat, clinging onto the phone as if it were his only remaining connection to the dim and distant real world.

His mind was clearly completely shredded. 'But the blood … it's everywhere. Oh Jesus! Shit. Shit. Shit.' He closed his eyes, breath coming in deep rasping gasps as his lungs battled to keep pace with the continued body shock.

Jackie ran back up the stairs two at a time, and walked straight into the empty bathroom. As before, it was pristine and immaculate. No blood splattered walls or butchered human remains existed. Perfect.

Daniel's frantic holler broke her moment of smug self-satisfaction. 'What do you think? What do you think? Reckon he topped himself?'

As one of the planets most pre-eminent figures in a secretive and dark entertainment format known as mind control, Jackie was fighting not to let her real emotion betray itself to him. Her fame across continental Europe and North America knew no bounds, yet in her homeland, she was still a relative unknown to all but a handful of diehard fans. Her form of 'entertainment', shunned by the mainstream, was an arcane craft – a combination of suggestion, psychology, showmanship, manipulation and a small sprinkling of magic. Within the closely guarded inner circles of her profession, she had been labelled 'maverick, dark, brooding and potentially dangerous – there is no place here for such malevolent trickery.' Such was the potency of her dark powers of suggestion, the merest physical touch of another human was all she needed to penetrate and manipulate their subconscious psyche.

Shunned by the media at home, her special brand of entertaining others quickly escaped the underground cult followings abroad, attaining instant mainstream success, with syndication deals across the world.

'Daniel!' she yelled. 'Come back up here! I think you've been working too hard.'

'No way! I'm calling the police.' By now, his voice had become a whimper, driven by angst, fright and curiosity.

'Daniel, there is no corpse up here. I do believe your imagination is getting the better of you.' She admired the way she was able to sound so calm and deadpan, yet goading him all the same.

'WHAT?' hesitating anger once again suddenly surfaced in his voice, her taunt lighting the fuse.

'As I said, take a look for yourself ...'

Thundering up the stairs, legs connecting each step with the force of a piston ramming into a borehole, the confused, frightened and angry young reptile barged back into the bathroom.

Despite a distinct lack of direct family or offspring in her life, Jackie fancied a change, hence the house hunting. A new $10m contract for a six week summer stint in Las Vegas had been signed, sealed and delivered with a cool $1 million advance to guarantee her signature. That advance was now safely banked and burning a serious hole in her pocket.

America had fallen in love with the notion of a female dark magician, breaking the sacred domination of the male in such a small and secretive population. She was well on her way to becoming one of the most powerful entertainment industry figures on the planet. But not right now.

'BUT THAT JUST CANNOT BE!' Daniel screamed, utterly dumbfounded at the sight of a now sparkling clean, diamond white bathroom suite. 'THE BLOOD ... HIS FACE ... THE WATER ...' he sank to his knees as he screamed; the first tiny convulsions of an imminent, yet involuntary vomiting episode evident in his movements. 'It was all there.'

He whispered to his shaking hands, 'It … was … all … there …'

Briefly, Jackie wondered if planting such a horrendous image into his gullible immature mind was stepping too far over the line. After all, the shock could kill him, especially after such a *sudden* insertion and removal. But then again, he was such a loathsome little toad …

'It just cannot be. What's happening to … me?' Daniel passed out, hitting his head on the porcelain rim of the toilet bowl as he slumped. Subsequently, as an added humiliation, his final resting place guaranteed he lay at an awkward angle, half suspended between the toilet and the linoleum floor, one arm unconsciously gripping the porcelain bowl as his head gently lolled from the edge of the rim as he began an over-animated, tortured groan. When viewed from the outside looking in, he was a grotesque vision of a youth gone mad on a binge drinking session, now paying the all too familiar price we all experience at some point in our lives – the dreaded chat with God on the porcelain telephone.

Her mischief – or was it retribution? – had worked perfectly. Double checking him for a pulse despite his self-pitying moans, she was satisfied he hadn't died of fright. Interestingly, his hair was now a silvery shade of grey – another imminent apocalyptic shock to his system. He would be in this state for quite some time.

Stepping over his prone form, Jackie whispered gently in his ear. 'I'll see myself out then. Thanks for your time. It's been … enlightening.' A wry smile spread across her face as she closed the front door behind her, leaving his groans to echo in isolation. As she began walking along the leafy, tree-lined street, she felt a deep sense of irony that an estate agent of all people had been able to put such a spring in her step and a smile on her face.

The Tea Doctor

For the fourth consecutive evening that week, falling into the sequence of being the fifth week that month, she placed her head in her hands, wracked with frustration and an ever penetrating, deepening concern.

'Joseph, will you *please* stop playing with your food and just … eat … it.' Her voice prickled in unison with the wayward rolling of her eyes into her head, adding to the visual representation of her despair. Once again, the evening meal had become a pantomime for Emily and her seven year old son.

'I don't like it. I'm not hungry,' the youngster muttered matter-of-factly into his plate of rapidly cooling pasta bolognaise, refusing to meet his mother's stare. 'You haven't eaten anything at home all week!' she spluttered, voice rising with every syllable. 'What don't you like about it all of a sudden? You've never complained before.' Even to the young boy, her angst-ridden desperation could barely be hidden. She was truly at the edge of her senses.

'I just don't.' His monosyllabic reply cut through her, as she noted how his eyes were darting uncontrollably to the left and right in a rapid fire movement whilst he concentrated as best he could on anything and everything in the room except for the plate before him and the traumatised visage of his mother.

'Well … what *do* you like? You've got to eat something.' Mild melancholy in her softly crackling voice betrayed the possibility that she may have been contemplating defeat.

'Chocolate!' He beamed in the knowledge that his tactic was working – she would give in soon, he just had to be patient.

'No Way!' she growled, bristling with indignation, determined to remain strong, refusing to give in to his quasi demand. 'Then I don't want anything,' he huffed, returning his undivided interest to the now congealing pile of goo underneath his nose, suddenly taking a great interest in the hand painted flower borders imprinted onto the ceramic plate.

This was not in the plan. It had never been in the script before. She always gave up – usually immediately. All he normally had to do was hang on for long enough, refuse to engage her in meaningful dialogue, and, Ta Dah! It never failed! Tonight, something was wrong, she never, ever, ever said no to him. Things were going critical by the second …

'Fine. Then I'm making an appointment for you to see Dr Webster first thing tomorrow morning. This can't go on.'

Things were going from seriously bad to disastrously worse. Where was this new found inner strength coming from? Who or what was giving her the gumption to resist his demands? He had to act quickly to avert disaster.

'Not going can't make me.' Maintaining his ability to not look his mother directly in the eye, he began poking the messy mass of rubbery pasta tubes, carving a swirling pattern in them as his finger squelched through in a wide circular motion.

'It's not fair.' He quietly mumbled, yet audible enough to be heard. 'Stop that right now!' Emily cried, her voice rising to a desperate shrill once more. 'That is a disgusting thing to do. Wait till I tell your father about this.'

Such a warning bore no effect on the increasingly petulant child, as on the rare occasions he actually spent time with his estranged father, his whims and demands – no matter how outrageous – were always met by a weak-willed grown up who would do anything for a quiet life.

'He lets me eat chocolate when I want. Don't care. Call him.'

Noisily dropping her knife and fork to her own half full plate, tolerance barrier for such antics finally breached, her hands slammed onto the pine table top, immediately commanding his full attention. 'I'll … I'll …'

'You'll what?' Joseph goaded, raising his head, eyes locking on to hers in an extraordinary act of defiance. His wicked, knowing smile was the ultimate act of mockery – he was successfully regaining control of the situation, as he usually did. Suddenly, inspiration slammed into her as if it were falling from the sky in torrents.

'I *won't* call the doctor!' Emma replied, a sly confident smile now breaking across *her* face. Little did the boy know, but she was about to successfully outplay him at his own game. 'I'll call the Tea Doctor instead!' she confidently proclaimed.

Tea Doctor? This was a new one. He had never heard of such a thing before. This could be a serious, unknown threat. Once again, he was on the ropes, needing to quickly gain the upper hand. 'Don't believe you. You're making it up.' As he spoke, Emily suddenly stood, quickly traversing the length of the kitchen to scoop up her mobile phone from the sideboard.

Returning to her chair, facing him once more, phone raised triumphantly above her head, the grittiness in her voice betrayed a growing confidence in her strategy. 'Eat!' she growled, 'Or else I'm calling him …'

'NO! I don't like it! I don't believe you!' Even as the words forcibly fell from his mouth, he knew she was gaining strength from his uncertainty. He was allowing his defences to crack – it was time to get a grip. Placing his index finger back into the gooey mess that was once a palatable pasta dish, he composed himself, concentrating as he took the ultimate stance of resistance.

'I don't believe you.'

Without responding, Emily calmly, slowly lowered her arm, allowing the small, illuminated screen of the phone to lie in the direct line of sight of her stubborn offspring. Watching patiently as he slowly formed the words and mouthed them to himself in a whisper in that way only young children do, she sensed the tide was finally turning her way in this latest instalment of their battle of wills.

Joseph tried to comprehend the display before him. 'Tea Doctor: 47948.' Silently mouthing the words several times over, she was unsure if he was in shock or just buying time to think of a suitable response. Despite this, a new found confidence surged through her. The tables were finally turning, and the sensation made her feel incredibly proud. Not only for inventing the 'Tea Doctor' in the first place – stroke of genius that it was – but also for being dexterous enough to punch in a random sequence of numbers into the directory menu of the phone, demonstrating the possibility of his existence, without Joseph even remotely noticing.

'He's not for real. I don't believe you.' To give him credit, the kid was stubborn and resilient. Not too unlike his mother.

'Oh, he's for real – would you like me to call him *right now?*'

'Yeah … I mean No. I mean …' Emma cupped a hand to her mouth, hiding the sly grin of victory.

Stalemate. The game was almost up. She was close now. He was running out of ideas. She was winning. The shame of it! One last roll of the dice was all he had left in him. Time to gamble.

'Go on then. Call him!' The cat was out of the bag. She had to put up or shut up now. In calling her bluff, he knew it could all blow up in her face, and yet, he still could not *completely* believe this Tea Doctor existed. Could he?

Joseph's uncertainty intensified when she punched the small buttons without flinching. 'Hello?' She cleared her throat to speak clearly to the unseen voice at the other end of the line. 'Is this the Tea Doctor?' She nodded at the invisible respondent, accentuating the illusion of a real conversation.

Damn! The game was up! She was talking to him right now! Still, she had only won her first battle – the war would continue to rage. For now though, he needed to climb down and comply. He would lick his wounds and regroup later on whilst he played in his room.

'It's my son, Joseph. He refuses to eat *anything* that I make him for tea every night.' Another faked pause. 'That's right, *every* night!' she emphasised, deliberately dragging her words.

Desperation crept into his thoughts. How could this happen? Shock commanded his irrational actions in the knowledge of defeat. 'You're making it up!' Joseph blurted. 'There's no one there!'

Ignoring him, Emily continued holding her nerve. 'What's more, he's being very, very rude, and making his mum very sad.' She briefly paused, thinking through her next fabricated piece of speech. The sudden silence in the kitchen cut into her like a razor blade. Her son looked utterly defeated, forlornly holding his fork – yet she had to finish it convincingly – the next words spoken to the non existent 'Tea Doctor' needed to be good. 'Can you come to the house and see him tonight please?' A pause coupled with the slightest hint of a whimper from Joseph's direction spurred her on.

'Yes, yes, late, after bedtime is fine. If I have to wake him up for you to see him it's not a problem.'

Disaster. She had actually done it. No point in arguing now, just get on with it, but make a fuss anyway.

'Nooooooo!' he screeched, spearing the first pasta tube with his fork, ramming it into his mouth, theatrically pulling faces, and chewing with enough force to crack his teeth.

'Too late,' Emily mouthed silently at him, unable to conceal her huge, triumphant grin in the process. 'It's not fair!' the apoplectic youngster bellowed, albeit forcing another morsel of cold food into his mouth immediately.

'OK then Tea Doctor, we'll see you later.' Pressing the red button to terminate the 'call', Emily's heart sang in unabashed pride. This particular performance, along with its stunning result, must surely be worthy of an Oscar nomination.

Facing her son once more, she could not help but feel a slight pang of guilt whilst watching his distressed features struggle with the odious task of forcing the now undesirable, gungy, gloopy meal into his resisting mouth. His face betrayed a billion emotions, yet he had been defeated, so had no choice other than to play along now – the potential threat of the Tea Doctor needed to be avoided at all costs. Miserably, he ate in silence, making the odd, retching and groaning noise, just to reassure his mother of the misery she was inflicting upon him.

Eventually, twenty minutes from the start of the whole episode, he placed the last piece of intact pasta on his tongue, closed his eyes and swallowed, as if he were taking a particularly nasty medicine.

There. It's all over. Break the silence, get out of here, lick your wounds, plot your revenge. Tomorrow is another day.

Neatly placing his knife and fork on the now empty plate, he finally spoke. 'There. All finished now. OK?'

'Fine! Well done! See, it wasn't *too* difficult – was it?'

Was she gloating? How on earth could she say it wasn't too difficult? It had been torture at its absolute worst. Still, he had to play it carefully – for the moment anyway.

'What does the Tea Doctor do?' There was an uncertain edginess in his cautious whisper. Yet Emily had been waiting for it, mentally running through her response whilst he made such a fuss over eating his meal.

'He places a spell on all children he visits.' The boy's eyes widened to the shape of saucers as his breath stopped in his throat. 'You see Joseph, the Tea Doctor is magic. It makes him cross when upset mums and dads have to call him because their children won't eat their tea.' She sounded so convincing; she was beginning to believe in her own story now.

That can't be right. Surely? How can that be allowed to happen these days? Need to get a grip – she might actually be telling the truth.

'Why does he put a spell on children? Are they bad spells?'

'He does it to make children eat properly. It's not nice, and he knows that, but he knows that children get ill when they don't eat properly.'

'What do you mean – *not nice*? Is the spell bad? Is it scary?'

'The spell is *horrible*. He places it on all children who are naughty eaters, making them want to eat one thing, and one thing only, until they become grown ups.'

This is too much. Resistance is futile – just take your punishment and move on.

'What's that?' Joseph, with every reserve of bravery and insolence long dissolved, was now distinctly alarmed.

'Worms!' Emily cackled, gaining a perverse pleasure from the ever increasing height of her tall tale. 'He waves a cane belching foul smelling green smoke, whilst chanting the spell. Finally, he breaks the invisible 'child time clock' that all children have; taking away their choice in the food you eat until you are grown up. That's when you are cursed for the rest of childhood to eat nothing but worms. It's horrid.'

Clamping a hand over his mouth, fighting the urge to be sick, eyes bulging he repeated just one word. 'WORMS?'

'Yeah! Live ones at that, so you can feel them wriggling in your mouth! He chews them up a little himself first, and then drops them into your mouth whilst you are sleeping ...' She paused, sensing and seeing his genuine fright. Had she taken things just a little too far? It *was* cruel to lay it on so thick, and yet ...

'And all because you won't eat properly Joseph.'

It was no good. With his defences completely eradicated, he was unable to hold back. Uncontrollable sobs of fear gripped him, rivulets of tears tumbling down his cheeks. 'I don't want the Tea Doctor coming here! I don't want to eat worms!' His wailing grew in intensity and volume, driven by angst and uncertainty.

Knowing that she had totally overstepped the mark by getting carried away, her imagination a little *too* emboldened for a seven year old boy – no matter how insolent – Emily moved quickly to clam the situation, her sense of guilt slowly suffocating as she gently spoke.

'If you go to bed on time tonight, without fuss, and go straight to sleep, I'll call him back and cancel the appointment.'

'Promise?' his reddening eyes pleaded through the tears.

'I promise. But you must behave at bedtime.' Although trying to calm him from his building distress, bedtime was the other traditional battleground on a nightly basis, and she rightfully felt there was an opportunity to change his habits here too – despite the extremity of her methods.

That night, for the first time in nearly two years, Joseph went to bed, on time, without resistance or fuss. Equally refreshing, there had been no tantrums involving cleaning teeth or putting on pyjamas, no excessive demands for extra bedtime stories, and no smuggling of toys to play with underneath the duvet once he was alone in the room.

Now, one and a half hours later, standing in his bedroom doorway, watching Joseph's peaceful, sleeping form, Emily felt nothing but all-consuming love, tinged with a healthy dose of shame at the manner in which she had frozen his heart with fear. Still, there was no denying that the Tea Doctor had proven to be a very persuasive method indeed – for now. Next time, she would be a little less graphic.

A sudden, loud bang on the front door from outside jolted her senses into automatic apprehension. It was 9.30, who on earth could it be at this time of the night? Why were they not ringing the doorbell?

Another loud thud followed by muffled scratching jarred her nerves further. Tiptoeing to the living room curtains, heart pounding and nerves crackling, she gently pulled them back, allowing the merest sliver of cold darkness outside to penetrate the light and security of the warm indoors. Unable to see the front door from her angle inside, hampered by the broken streetlight glowing eerily like a fractured, redundant lighthouse, all she could see were long, jittery shadows casting a sinister presence across the small front garden, and a small car, dark in colour, parked in the street beyond, its make and model indistinguishable. A silhouetted figure sat motionless in the driver's seat, as a small roof mounted beacon emanated a random, eerie luminous green, casting an intermittent emerald spotlight on the houses opposite. Emily's breathing became ragged and sharp, her heart crashing against the inside of her ribcage. There was a doctor on call parked outside.

For a third time, a knock on the door, forcefully now, impatient and malevolent. Sensing uncertainty, goose bumps prickling her flesh, Emily shuffled to the front door. There was no choice – even if she needed to call for help, the telephone was located in the small porch adjacent to the aforementioned door.

Upon hesitantly reaching the white panelled, UPVC portal, her conscious rationale immediately confirmed she was right to be wary, even nervous. Her subconsciousness was already screaming, the physical wail firmly stuck in her throat.

Enormous grey and brown earthworms pooled over the bristle entrance mat, slithering and writhing en mass from the letterbox to the floor below. As fronds of stench-ridden dark green smoke crept through the hinge side gap between the door and its frame, Emily maintained her frantic, silent scream, as shock kept her firmly rooted to the spot. Then came the voice, inhuman and foreboding.

'Doctor's here!' the low guttural growl shook the floor she stood on as yet more worms were forced through the letterbox by a clawed, leathery three fingered hand. 'Someone here call a doctor! … Open up, open up, whoever you are!'

Worms continued to fall, the voice continued to mock, and the door began to splinter and crack under the force of the blows from the thing on the other side.

'Doctor's in!' it cackled, as the door finally gave way under the brutal assault, imploding into thousands of tiny plastic shards.

It wouldn't be long now. Not long at all.

Killing Santa

As with any other playground spat between highly agitated ten year old boys, there was a chief tormentor, and a baying crowd of cronies, howling in derision at the victim, who in turn usually stood encircled in the middle of it all, well and truly on the receiving end of the spite.

Raymond was the object of this particular bout of nastiness, instigated by the classroom thug, Frederick. He stood his ground manfully, tortured yet ignorant of his increasingly intimidating surroundings. It wasn't the spiteful taunts of Frederick, laughing and goading the others as he spoke. It wasn't even the presence of the assorted cronies surrounding him, chanting a rhythmic mockery designed to inflict maximum distress to his psyche. It was something far worse – a feeling of deception and betrayal – inflicted upon him by a loved one.

Eventually, the bell signalling the end of lunch had his tormentors running for the classroom. Yet for Raymond, the turmoil within remained, and the bullies were in no way the symptom or the cause.

Long after the taunts of 'Fairy Boy', 'Baby Boy' and 'Girlie' had subsided into his distant memory, fading with the passing of the school day; Raymond was completely unable to grasp his new found knowledge – the original source of the cruel yet largely ignored playground taunts. He was yet to know or understand it, but his life was to change forever on that day.

Upon the piercing, shrill din of the electronic bell signalling the end of yet another academic day, Raymond left the classroom sluggishly, dragging his heels as he made his way to the brightly painted green steel gates and welcoming smile of his mother. Only today, his heavy heart had plunged his sense of trust and integrity deep into his black leather shoes.

'See you tomorrow fairy boy!' Frederick whispered as the massed throng of children traversed the evening rush hour playground, unheard and unseen by the waiting gaggle of parents beyond. Raymond deliberately failed to respond, choosing to ignore his antagonist, conserving his energies and bravery for an altogether bigger conversation when he got home.

'Good afternoon, sir!' his beaming mother cheerily greeted with a smile that could easily compete with a sixty watt light bulb any time.

Raymond merely mumbled an unenthusiastic 'Hi', failing to make any effort to look beyond the damp grey concrete at his feet. As is the case of all caring mothers, she instantaneously sensed a problem, and immediately her heart skipped a beat in pure anguish. She made the split second decision to let it go for the moment – concentrate instead on the half mile stroll home – where she could burrow into whatever issue existed in the sanctuary and privacy of their own four walls.

Throughout that entire silent walk through the late December dusk, where night meets day before teatime and the streetlights stay on for twenty-four hours, Raymond was sullen and uncommunicative, unusually subdued for a boy who normally exuded energy and excitement, especially at this time of the year.

Once safely indoors with the front door firmly closed, shutting out the vast array of imperfections loitering in the outside world, Raymond immediately met his mother's gaze and broke his awkward silence.

'I don't know how to tell you this ...' Tears formed in the corners of his sparkling green eyes.

Before he had a chance to continue, his mother adopted a soothing, compassionate stance to make him feel easy. 'It's OK. If you're in trouble, it's easier to get it out into the open now. Don't worry, just tell me.'

Raymond swiped at the stinging tears, brushing them from his eyes and cheeks, annoyed at her mistaken assumption that actually a million miles away from what he was *really* bothered about.

'I'm not in trouble,' he murmured.

'Then what is it honey?' Panic tinged her voice now, frustrated he wasn't getting to the point of his distress quickly enough. She gently stroked his soft red cheek, as if encouraging the words to spill out automatically.

'It's just …' He took a deep breath, still fighting his reflexive urges to sob. 'It's just that I'm not sure if I believe in Santa any more.'

Her hand limply fell away as if she had been shot in the arm. The entire house perished under the deathly silence that followed. Such was the shock of his statement; time itself seemed to momentarily stop. Shock rocked her trembling voice as she responded in the only way she could muster.

'Why do you say that? What's happened?' Guilt pricked at her, generating discomforting sensations akin to lying on a bed of rotting thorns. Sensing her shock provided him with an opportunity to speak, so he continued.

'Frederick and his friends started shouting on the playground at the start of lunchtime … going on about how Santa wasn't real, and that the presents come from your mum and dad, who put them out when you're asleep.' His forlorn gaze never left his feet whilst he spoke, unable to look his mother in the eye.

As she attempted a response, the fragmented distress in her voice told him everything – a shocking truth he wished he had never discovered. 'What did you say to them darling?' She was on edge, her voice a crackled whisper, an abyss of guilt and sudden exposure threatening to swallow her whole.

'I defended Santa. For a bit, anyway …' Raising his head slowly, he suddenly felt the strength needed to look her direct in the eye. 'But I'm not sure now.'

His silent plea, willing her to tell him that Frederick and his cronies were wrong, that 'Of course Santa is real, and you were right to stand up for him', never came. She couldn't do it. She couldn't lie to him any more. Even though this lie would defend a lie that had existed for years, she couldn't bear to be the one finally shattering his beliefs. Her obvious discomfort – a discomfort last experienced two years previously when he asked that other immortal childhood question of where babies originate from – betrayed the truth.

Sitting there, holding her breath in order to avoid the temptation to speak, she knew they had reached a milestone, a rite of passage moment, this one being where her son began the fraught journey in crossing the gap between childhood and adolescence.

'He's not real, is he?' Raymond finally spoke, with a conviction and gravity indicating not a question, but a statement of fact.

Reaching out, she put her arms around him, sobbing with guilt and shame. 'So it was a lie.' He shuffled away from her embrace. 'You've been lying to me all this time.'

They sat together, again in silence as he worked out everything in his ten year old mind. She wished she could make things better, but knew it impossible. Not only was she unable to fix this permanent break, but fighting the demons of guilt continued to absorb her. Had she been the cause of this in the first place? After all, Father Christmas is just a great big lie all parents tell their children from earliest infancy. Who could blame Raymond for thinking that if she'd lied about this, what else was she capable of lying about?

'So that's it then.' He looked at her once more, his red eyes now devoid of tears. How dare adults tell children lying is wrong, that the truth is always right. The truth hurts. Hard.

'What's it, darling?'

'Things will never be the same mum. It's always going to be so different …' He stood up, moving away from her. Pausing for the briefest of seconds, he left the room with a cursory glance in her direction, and then bounded up the stairs, loudly slamming his bedroom door without uttering a word.

In that moment, her sense of the magic of Christmas evaporated. It was then, the realization that a huge part of Christmas was founded on being able to believe once again, through the eyes of her own child – was now gone for eternity. For the second time in her life, the point in which she once knew the truth with her head, had given way to what she felt in her heart. And once again, it had been taken.

The lines between knowing and unknowing, between belief and unbelief, so wondrously blurred since Raymond had been a baby, were gone.

For the millionth time that Christmas, as hundreds of thousands of children all over the planet discovered the truth, Santa passed away, slain by the brutal reality of a sharp tongue, hand in hand with the burden of inevitability.